The Last Oblivion
Best Fantastic Poems of
Clark Ashton Smith

Edited by S. T. Joshi and David E. Schultz

Hippocampus Press

New York

Copyright © 2002 by Hippocampus Press
Introduction and editorial matter
copyright © 2002 by S. T. Joshi and David E. Schultz

Published by Hippocampus Press
P.O. Box 641, New York, NY 10156.
www.hippocampuspress.com

Permission to publish the text and artwork has been granted by
CASiana, the Estate of Clark Ashton Smith.
The artwork by Clark Ashton Smith on page 3 is used by
permission of Scott Connors. All other artwork by
Clark Ashton Smith is used by permission of Mara Kirk Hart.

The photograph of Clark Ashton Smith on the back cover is used by
permission of Alan H. Teague and The Literary Estate of Emil Petaja.

Cover design by Barbara Briggs Silbert.
Hippocampus Press logo designed by Anastasia Damianakos.

All rights reserved.
No part of this work may be reproduced in any form or by any means
without the written permission of the publisher.

First Edition
1 3 5 7 9 8 6 4 2

ISBN 0-9673215-5-7

Contents

Introduction   9
  A Note on the Text   12
  Acknowledgments   12
The Hashish-Eater; or, The Apocalypse of Evil   15
I. The Star-Treader   30
  The Star-Treader   30
  Ode to the Abyss   33
  Nirvana   35
  The Song of a Comet   36
  Lament of the Stars   38
  In Saturn   40
  Triple Aspect   40
  The Abyss Triumphant   41
  The Motes   41
  Desire of Vastness   42
  Shadows   42
  A Dream of the Abyss   43
  After Armageddon   44
  The Ancient Quest   45
  A Dream of Oblivion   45
  Ode to Light   46
  Ode to Matter   47
II. Medusa and Other Horrors   49
  Nero   49
  Medusa   51
  Averted Malefice   52
  The Medusa of the Skies   53
  Saturn   53
  In Lemuria   60
  Satan Unrepentant   60
  The Ghoul and the Seraph   63
  The Medusa of Despair   67
  A Vision of Lucifer   67
  The Witch in the Graveyard   68
  The Flight of Azrael   70
  The Mummy   71
  Minatory   72
  To the Chimera   72
  The Whisper of the Worm   73

The Envoys	73
Nyctalops	74
Jungle Twilight	76
Necromancy	76
The Witch with Eyes of Amber	77
Cambion	77
The Saturnienne	78
Chance	79
Revenant	79
Song of the Necromancer	81
Pour chercher du nouveau	82
Witch-Dance	83
Not Theirs the Cypress-Arch	84
III. THE ELDRITCH DARK	**85**
A Song from Hell	85
The Titans in Tartarus	86
The Twilight Woods	88
Lethe	89
Atlantis	89
The Eldritch Dark	89
White Death	90
A Dead City	90
The Cloud-Islands	91
The City of the Titans	92
The City of Destruction	92
Beyond the Great Wall	93
Solution	94
Rosa Mystica	94
Symbols	95
The City in the Desert	95
The Melancholy Pool	96
Twilight on the Snow	96
The Land of Evil Stars	97
Memnon at Midnight	98
The Kingdom of Shadows	98
Moon-Dawn	100
Outlanders	100
Warning	100
The Nightmare Tarn	101
The Prophet Speaks	102
The Outer Land	103
In Thessaly	105
Le Miroir des blanches fleurs	106
The Moonlight Desert	107
Ougabalys	107
Desert Dweller	108

Amithaine	109
The Dark Chateau	110
Averoigne	111
Zothique	112
IV. SAID THE DREAMER	**114**
The Castle of Dreams	114
The Dream-God's Realm	114
Imagination	115
The Last Night	118
Shadow of Nightmare	118
A Song of Dreams	119
The Dream-Bridge	120
Said the Dreamer	120
Dolor of Dreams	121
Luna Aeternalis	122
Echo of Memnon	123
Nightmare	123
The Last Goddess	124
Love Malevolent	124
The Wingless Archangels	125
Enchanted Mirrors	125
Selenique	126
Maya	126
Fantaisie d'Antan	127
In Slumber	128
V. THE REFUGE OF BEAUTY	**129**
The Power of Eld	129
Strangeness	129
The Nereid	130
Exotique	131
Transcendence	131
The Tears of Lilith	132
Cleopatra	132
The Refuge of Beauty	133
Sandalwood	133
The Last Oblivion	134
Alienage	135
Adventure	136
Interrogation	137
Canticle	138
To Antares	138
Connaissance	139
Exorcism	139
Lamia	140
Farewell to Eros	141

Some Blind Eidolon   142
Bacchante   143
Resurrection   144
The Sorcerer to His Love   145
The Hill of Dionysus   145
Midnight Beach   147
Omniety   147
VI. TO THE DARKNESS   **149**
Ode on Imagination   149
Retrospect and Forecast   151
To the Darkness   151
A Dream of Beauty   152
The Pursuer   153
In the Desert   153
The Nameless Wraith   154
To the Daemon of Sublimity   155
Desolation   155
Inferno   156
Dissonance   156
Remembered Light   156
The Incubus of Time   157
Laus Mortis   158
The Hope of the Infinite   158
Antepast   159
Forgotten Sorrow   159
Lunar Mystery   160
The Funeral Urn   160
Mors   161
September   161
Ennui   162
VII. THE SORCERER DEPARTS   **163**
To Omar Khayyam   163
To Nora May French   165
On Re-reading Baudelaire   167
To George Sterling: A Valediction   168
To Howard Phillips Lovecraft   170
H. P. L.   171
Soliloquy in a Ebon Tower   171
Cycles   174
GLOSSARY   **175**
BIBLIOGRAPHY   **179**
INDEX OF TITLES   **187**
INDEX OF FIRST LINES   **191**

INTRODUCTION

That Clark Ashton Smith (1893–1961) is one of the premier American poets of the twentieth century is an assertion that would evoke reactions ranging from bemusement to scorn in the general literary and academic community, but this has more to do with the tendencies—some might say vagaries—of twentieth-century poetry than with any putative deficiencies on Smith's part. That the verbally complex and metrically strict poetry of Smith is out of place amidst the deliberate obscurity of T. S. Eliot, the deliberate prosaicism of William Carlos Williams, and the deliberate looseness of the confessional poets is a truism; but it is equally a truism that Smith draws upon, and thereby extends, the heritage of English and American poetry—from Milton to Swinburne, from Shelley to George Sterling—thus linking himself with poetic history in a way that makes his Modernist contemporaries and successors seem hollow and rootless.

This is not the place for a full-scale analysis of Smith's poetry—an analysis that cannot be written until the entire corpus of his verse, published and unpublished, is made available. It will suffice here to trace the broadest outlines of Smith's work as a poet, so that readers can appreciate his lifelong fascination with a literary mode that brought him only fleeting celebrity and only minimal monetary benefit. Smith may be better known to enthusiasts of horror and fantasy literature for his exotic tales of weirdness and wonder, but the great majority of those tales were written in a mere half-decade (1930-35), and for most of his literary career he had no thought of being a fiction writer; but his devotion to poetry remained constant from earliest childhood to his final days.

When A. M. Robertson published Smith's *The Star-Treader and Other Poems* in the summer of 1912, readers and critics alike hailed the nineteen-year-old from central California as a poetic prodigy on the order of Keats and Shelley. Few, however, were aware of how much a prodigy Smith really was, for some of the poems in that volume dated to his fourteenth year. The volume would not have been published had Smith not initiated, the year previous, an intense and fruitful correspondence with George Sterling, then the reigning literary figure of San Francisco. Sterling's own "star-poem," *The Testimony of the Suns* (1903), perhaps influenced Smith's own ventures into the poetry of the heavens, but Sterling himself acknowledged that the pupil was well on his way to eclipsing his master. The reaction to *The Star-Treader* had all the makings of a nine-days' wonder—similar to that inspired by Ambrose Bierce's lauding of Sterling's poem, "A Wine of Wizardry," in 1907—but Smith was no poetic flash in the pan. Although six years passed before his next volume, *Odes and Sonnets,* appeared, he devoted himself unremittingly to poetry; and it is fitting that that volume of 1918 was published by the prestigious Book Club of California.

But just as Sterling himself never fully achieved nationwide recognition, content with being a West Coast literary phenomenon, Smith had difficulty translating his early celebrity into general recognition. Both *Ebony and Crystal* (1922) and *Sandalwood* (1925) were "privately published," funded largely by Sterling and Donald Wandrei, respectively. They received relatively little attention even in California, and Smith would not publish another volume of poetry until 1937.

The publication of *Ebony and Crystal* approximately coincided with Smith's initial contact with H. P. Lovecraft; and it is scarcely to be doubted that his attempts at writing fantastic fiction, begun a few years later, were inspired by Lovecraft's *example,* if not by any of Lovecraft's actual stories. No doubt Smith found the income generated by publication of his tales in the pulp magazines of great benefit as he tended to his increasingly ailing parents; but it is also not to be doubted that the death of his mother and father, in 1935 and 1937 respectively, freed Smith from the need to be a pulpsmith and allowed him to return to the unremunerative career of poet.

The founding of Arkham House in 1939 by August Derleth and Donald Wandrei proved quickly beneficial to Smith, as several volumes of his tales appeared in rapid succession; but Smith never saw the publication of what surely must be regarded as the capstone of his literary career, *Selected Poems* (1971), whose assemblage he had completed in 1949. Instead, Derleth mollified Smith by issuing slim collections of his later verse—*The Dark Chateau* (1951) and *Spells and Philtres* (1958). These volumes prove that the spectacular imagination of his fiery youth had been harnessed and broadened, leavened by an awareness of the complexity of human emotion face to face with the boundless cosmos. After his death, Smith's literary executor Roy A. Squires published a considerable portion of his unpublished poetry, most notably the cycle *The Hill of Dionysus* (1962), but much remains uncollected or unpublished.

To segregate the "fantastic" poetry from Smith's overall poetic corpus may seem a highly artificial undertaking, for the element of the bizarre pervades his entire oeuvre in numerous and complex ways. Nevertheless, a certain segment of his verse can legitimately be said to contain a more concentrated dose of the weird than others, and this volume presents a sheaf of Smith's fantastic poetry arranged in broad thematic categories. The fashioning of these categories is itself a problematic undertaking, and should be regarded merely as suggestive rather than definitive. At the head of the volume, fittingly, is Smith's masterpiece of fantasy, *The Hashish-Eater* (1920), perhaps the most sustained expression of cosmicism in all literature. Following this epic, the first section presents Smith's other ventures into poetic cosmicism—the keynote of *The Star-Treader,* from which many of the poems are drawn. Section II contains poems about fantastic creatures, ranging from the sociopathic horror of the Emperor Nero to the mythic terrors of Medusa and the Titans. In Section III we find poems on exotic landscapes—a topos particularly close to Smith's heart, and one that perhaps most closely links his verse to his fantastic tales; it is no surprise to see poems on Atlantis, Zothique, and Averoigne here. Section IV exhibits the dream-element that is central to so many of Smith's poems and stories. In Section V, poems that mingle weirdness and love are to be found. Much of Smith's purely amatory verse is of high merit, but in these poems the union of fantasy and the erotic presents a distinctive flavor found only in the very best of Sterling's verse. In Section VI, Smith's broodingly pessimistic or misanthropic poetry is displayed, while the final brief section contains his poems to his celebrated predecessors and contemporaries. Here we come upon two inexpressibly poignant elegies, "To George Sterling: A Valediction" (1926) and "To Howard Phillips Lovecraft" (1937).

The likelihood that Smith will ever attain widespread recognition for his poetry is, to be sure, not great. Most members of the general literary community have become so unaccustomed to the lushness and complexity of this kind of poetry that they are likely to pass it off unthinkingly as either esoteric or *passé* (as if literary merit were somehow equivalent to contemporaneousness); while devotees of Smith's fiction appear to be unfamiliar with the rhetoric of poetry and are therefore unused to fantasy in verse form. But to the judicious reader, the compressed brilliance, the imaginative range, and the verbal and metrical panache of Smith's odes, sonnets, and lyrics will be immediately evident. The Roman axiom *pulchrum est paucorum hominum* ("Beauty is for the few") never had a more relevant object than the poetry of Clark Ashton Smith.

—S. T. JOSHI
DAVID E. SCHULTZ

A Note on the Text

The text of this volume is based in large part on Smith's magnum opus, *Selected Poems,* prepared in 1944–49 but published only in 1971. Smith, having died ten years previously, did not live to see publication of this great work, which occurred more than twenty years after delivering the manuscript of the book. *Selected Poems* contains a number of errors, which have been corrected by consulting the typescript of *Selected Poems,* incorporating correct readings provided by Donald Sidney-Fryer, and consulting various manuscripts and published appearances of individual poems.

This volume contains several uncollected and previously unpublished poems, and early poems first published after Smith's death. The editors have made very minor changes to these early poems, to make them conform to Smith's practice in compiling *Selected Poems.* These pertain primarily to matters of spelling and non-indentation of rhyming lines.

Because Smith's verse is so verbally rich, full of recondite and *récherché* vocabulary, we have supplied a glossary of the more unusual words found in the poems.

Acknowledgments

Over the years, the assistance of many individuals has contributed to the growth of our knowledge of Smith and his work. Many have provided copies of rare and difficult to obtain appearances of his work. The editors would particularly like to thank Douglas A. Anderson, Steve Behrends, Scott Connors, Derrick Hussey, Stefan Dziemianowicz, Timothy Evans, Rah Hoffman, Harold Miller of the State Historical Society of Wisconsin, and Stuart David Schiff.

The study of the works and life of Clark Ashton Smith must begin with the pioneering work of Donald Sydney-Fryer. Bibliographer, biographer, textual scholar, critic, and a poet of no small attainment, Sidney-Fryer's scholarship is broad and deep. This edition owes much to the many aspects of his work.

The Last Oblivion

> . . . in some strange and latter planet, wrought
> From molten shards and meteor-dust of this,
> My hand shall pluck an unsuspected bloom . . .

The Hashish-Eater;
or, The Apocalypse of Evil

Bow down: I am the emperor of dreams;
I crown me with the million-colored sun
Of secret worlds incredible, and take
Their trailing skies for vestment when I soar,
Throned on the mounting zenith, and illume
The spaceward-flown horizon infinite.
Like rampant monsters roaring for their glut,
The fiery-crested oceans rise and rise,
By jealous moons maleficently urged
To follow me for ever; mountains horned
With peaks of sharpest adamant, and mawed
With sulphur-lit volcanoes lava-langued,
Usurp the skies with thunder, but in vain;
And continents of serpent-shapen trees,
With slimy trunks that lengthen league by league,
Pursue my flight through ages spurned to fire
By that supreme ascendance; sorcerers,
And evil kings, predominantly armed
With scrolls of fulvous dragon-skin whereon
Are worm-like runes of ever-twisting flame,
Would stay me; and the sirens of the stars,
With foam-like songs from silver fragrance wrought,
Would lure me to their crystal reefs; and moons
Where viper-eyed, senescent devils dwell,
With antic gnomes abominably wise,
Heave up their icy horns across my way.
But naught deters me from the goal ordained
By suns and eons and immortal wars,
And sung by moons and motes; the goal whose name
Is all the secret of forgotten glyphs
By sinful gods in torrid rubies writ
For ending of a brazen book; the goal
Whereat my soaring ecstasy may stand
In amplest heavens multiplied to hold

My hordes of thunder-vested avatars,
And Promethèan armies of my thought,
That brandish claspèd levins. There I call
My memories, intolerably clad
In light the peaks of paradise may wear,
And lead the Armageddon of my dreams
Whose instant shout of triumph is become
Immensity's own music: for their feet
Are founded on innumerable worlds,
Remote in alien epochs, and their arms
Upraised, are columns potent to exalt
With ease ineffable the countless thrones
Of all the gods that are or gods to be,
And bear the seats of Asmodai and Set
Above the seventh paradise.

                          Supreme
In culminant omniscience manifold,
And served by senses multitudinous,
Far-posted on the shifting walls of time,
With eyes that roam the star-unwinnowed fields
Of utter night and chaos, I convoke
The Babel of their visions, and attend
At once their myriad witness. I behold
In Ombos, where the fallen Titans dwell,
With mountain-builded walls, and gulfs for moat,
The secret cleft that cunning dwarves have dug
Beneath an alp-like buttress; and I list,
Too late, the clang of adamantine gongs
Dinned by their drowsy guardians, whose feet
Have felt the wasp-like sting of little knives
Embrued with slobber of the basilisk
Or the pail juice of wounded upas. In
Some red Antarean garden-world, I see
The sacred flower with lips of purple flesh,
And silver-lashed, vermilion-lidded eyes
Of torpid azure; whom his furtive priests
At moonless eve in terror seek to slay
With bubbling grails of sacrificial blood
That hide a hueless poison. And I read
Upon the tongue of a forgotten sphinx,

The annulling word a spiteful demon wrote
In gall of slain chimeras; and I know
What pentacles the lunar wizards use,
That once allured the gulf-returning roc,
With ten great wings of furlèd storm, to pause
Midmost an alabaster mount; and there,
With boulder-weighted webs of dragons' gut
Uplift by cranes a captive giant built,
They wound the monstrous, moonquake-throbbing bird,
And plucked from off his saber-taloned feet
Uranian sapphires fast in frozen blood,
And amethysts from Mars. I lean to read
With slant-lipped mages, in an evil star,
The monstrous archives of a war that ran
Through wasted eons, and the prophecy
Of wars renewed, which shall commemorate
Some enmity of wivern-headed kings
Even to the brink of time. I know the blooms
Of bluish fungus, freaked with mercury,
That bloat within the craters of the moon,
And in one still, selenic hour have shrunk
To pools of slime and fetor; and I know
What clammy blossoms, blanched and cavern-grown,
Are proffered to their gods in Uranus
By mole-eyed peoples; and the livid seed
Of some black fruit a king in Saturn ate,
Which, cast upon his tinkling palace-floor,
Took root between the burnished flags, and now
Hath mounted and become a hellish tree,
Whose lithe and hairy branches, lined with mouths,
Net like a hundred ropes his lurching throne,
And strain at starting pillars. I behold
The slowly-thronging corals that usurp
Some harbor of a million-masted sea,
And sun them on the league-long wharves of gold—
Bulks of enormous crimson, kraken-limbed
And kraken-headed, lifting up as crowns
The octiremes of perished emperors,
And galleys fraught with royal gems, that sailed
From a sea-fled haven.

                              Swifter and stranger grow
The visions: now a mighty city looms,
Hewn from a hill of purest cinnabar
To domes and turrets like a sunrise thronged
With tier on tier of captive moons, half-drowned
In shifting erubescence. But whose hands
Were sculptors of its doors, and columns wrought
To semblance of prodigious blooms of old,
No eremite hath lingered there to say,
And no man comes to learn: for long ago
A prophet came, warning its timid king
Against the plague of lichens that had crept
Across subverted empires, and the sand
Of wastes that cyclopean mountains ward;
Which, slow and ineluctable, would come
To take his fiery bastions and his fanes,
And quench his domes with greenish tetter. Now
I see a host of naked giants, armed
With horns of behemoth and unicorn,
Who wander, blinded by the clinging spells
Of hostile wizardry, and stagger on
To forests where the very leaves have eyes,
And ebonies like wrathful dragons roar
To teaks a-chuckle in the loathly gloom;
Where coiled lianas lean, with serried fangs,
From writhing palms with swollen boles that moan;
Where leeches of a scarlet moss have sucked
The eyes of some dead monster, and have crawled
To bask upon his azure-spotted spine;
Where hydra-throated blossoms hiss and sing,
Or yawn with mouths that drip a sluggish dew
Whose touch is death and slow corrosion. Then
I watch a war of pygmies, met by night,
With pitter of their drums of parrot's hide,
On plains with no horizon, where a god
Might lose his way for centuries; and there,
In wreathèd light and fulgors all convolved,
A rout of green, enormous moons ascend,
With rays that like a shivering venom run
On inch-long swords of lizard-fang.

                                    Surveyed
From this my throne, as from a central sun,
The pageantries of worlds and cycles pass;
Forgotten splendors, dream by dream, unfold
Like tapestry, and vanish; violet suns,
Or suns of changeful iridescence, bring
Their rays about me like the colored lights
Imploring priests might lift to glorify
The face of some averted god; the songs
Of mystic poets in a purple world
Ascend to me in music that is made
From unconceivèd perfumes and the pulse
Of love ineffable; the lute-players
Whose lutes are strung with gold of the utmost moon,
Call forth delicious languors, never known
Save to their golden kings; the sorcerers
Of hooded stars inscrutable to God,
Surrender me their demon-wrested scrolls,
Inscribed with lore of monstrous alchemies
And awful transformations.
                              If I will,
I am at once the vision and the seer,
And mingle with my ever-streaming pomps,
And still abide their suzerain: I am
The neophyte who serves a nameless god,
Within whose fane the fanes of Hecatompylos
Were arks the Titan worshippers might bear,
Or flags to pave the threshold; or I am
The god himself, who calls the fleeing clouds
Into the nave where suns might congregate
And veils the darkling mountain of his face
With fold on solemn fold; for whom the priests
Amass their monthly hecatomb of gems—
Opals that are a camel-cumbering load,
And monstrous alabraundines, won from war
With realms of hostile serpents; which arise,
Combustible, in vapors many-hued
And myrrh-excelling perfumes. It is I,
The king, who holds with scepter-dropping hand
The helm of some great barge of orichalchum,

Sailing upon an amethystine sea
To isles of timeless summer: for the snows
Of hyperborean winter, and their winds,
Sleep in his jewel-builded capital,
Nor any charm of flame-wrought wizardry,
Nor conjured suns may rout them; so he flees,
With captive kings to urge his serried oars,
Hopeful of dales where amaranthine dawn
Hath never left the faintly sighing lote
And lisping moly. Firm of heart, I fare
Impanoplied with azure diamond,
As hero of a quest Achernar lights,
To deserts filled with ever-wandering flames
That feed upon the sullen marl, and soar
To wrap the slopes of mountains, and to leap
With tongues intolerably lengthening
That lick the blenchèd heavens. But there lives
(Secure as in a garden walled from wind)
A lonely flower by a placid well,
Midmost the flaring tumult of the flames,
That roar as roars a storm-possessèd sea,
Impacable for ever; and within
That simple grail the blossom lifts, there lies
One drop of an incomparable dew
Which heals the parchèd weariness of kings,
And cures the wound of wisdom. I am page
To an emperor who reigns ten thousand years,
And through his labyrinthine palace-rooms,
Through courts and colonnades and balconies
Wherein immensity itself is mazed,
I seek the golden gorget he hath lost,
On which, in sapphires fine as orris-seed,
Are writ the names of his conniving stars
And friendly planets. Roaming thus, I hear
Like demon tears incessant, through dark ages,
The drip of sullen clepsydrae; and once
In every lustrum, hear the brazen clocks
Innumerably clang with such a sound
As brazen hammers make, by devils dinned
On tombs of all the dead; and nevermore

I find the gorget, but at length I find
A sealèd room whose nameless prisoner
Moans with a nameless torture, and would turn
To hell's red rack as to a lilied couch
From that whereon they stretched him; and I find,
Prostrate upon a lotus-painted floor,
The loveliest of all belovèd slaves
My emperor hath, and from her pulseless side
A serpent rises, whiter than the root
Of some venefic bloom in darkness grown,
And gazes up with green-lit eyes that seem
Like drops of cold, congealing poison.

                                      Hark!
What word was whispered in a tongue unknown,
In crypts of some impenetrable world?
Whose is the dark, dethroning secrecy
I cannot share, though I am king of suns,
And king therewith of strong eternity,
Whose gnomons with their swords of shadow guard
My gates, and slay the intruder? Silence loads
The wind of ether, and the worlds are still
To hear the word that flees mine audience.
In simultaneous ruin, all my dreams
Fall like a rack of fuming vapors raised
To semblance by a necromant, and leave
Spirit and sense unthinkably alone
Above a universe of shrouded stars
And suns that wander, cowled with sullen gloom,
Like witches to a Sabbath. . . . Fear is born
In crypts below the nadir, and hath crawled
Reaching the floor of space, and waits for wings
To lift it upward like a hellish worm
Fain for the flesh of cherubim. Red orbs
And eyes that gleam remotely as the stars,
But are not eyes of suns or galaxies,
Gather and throng to the base of darkness; a flame
Behind some black, abysmal curtain burns,
Implacable, and fanned to whitest wrath
By raisèd wings that flail the whiffled gloom,
And make a brief and broken wind that moans

As one who rides a throbbing rack. There is
A Thing that crouches, worlds and years remote,
Whose horns a demon sharpens, rasping forth
A note to shatter the donjon-keeps of time,
Or crack the sphere of crystal. All is dark
For ages, and my tolling heart suspends
Its clamor as within the clutch of death
Tightening with tense, hermetic rigors. Then,
In one enormous, million-flashing flame,
The stars unveil, the suns remove their cowls,
And beam to their responding planets; time
Is mine once more, and armies of its dreams
Rally to that insuperable throne
Firmed on the zenith.

     Once again I seek
The meads of shining moly I had found
In some anterior vision, by a stream
No cloud hath ever tarnished; where the sun,
A gold Narcissus, loiters evermore
Above his golden image. But I find
A corpse the ebbing water will not keep,
With eyes like sapphires that have lain in hell
And felt the hissing coals; and all the flowers
About me turn to hooded serpents, swayed
By flutes of devils in lascivious dance
Meet for the nod of Satan, when he reigns
Above the raging Sabbath, and is wooed
By sarabands of witches. But I turn
To mountains guarding with their horns of snow
The source of that befoulèd rill, and seek
A pinnacle where none but eagles climb,
And they with failing pennons. But in vain
I flee, for on that pylon of the sky
Some curse hath turned the unprinted snow to flame—
Red fires that curl and cluster to my tread,
Trying the summit's narrow cirque. And now
I see a silver python far beneath—
Vast as a river that a fiend hath witched
And forced to flow reverted in its course
To fountains whence it issued. Rapidly

It winds from slope to crumbling slope, and fills
Ravines and chasmal gorges, till the crags
Totter with coil on coil incumbent. Soon
It hath entwined the pinnacle I keep,
And gapes with a fanged, unfathomable maw
Wherein Great Typhon and Enceladus
Were orts of daily glut. But I am gone,
For at my call a hippogriff hath come,
And firm between his thunder-beating wings
I mount the sheer cerulean walls of noon
And see the earth, a spurnèd pebble, fall—
Lost in the fields of nether stars—and seek
A planet where the outwearied wings of time
Might pause and furl for respite, or the plumes
Of death be stayed, and loiter in reprieve
Above some deathless lily: for therein
Beauty hath found an avatar of flowers—
Blossoms that clothe it as a colored flame
From peak to peak, from pole to sullen pole,
And turn the skies to perfume. There I find
A lonely castle, calm, and unbeset
Save by the purple spears of amaranth,
And leafing iris tender-sworded. Walls
Of flushèd marble, wonderful with rose,
And domes like golden bubbles, and minarets
That take the clouds as coronal—these are mine,
For voiceless looms the peaceful barbican,
And the heavy-teethed portcullis hangs aloft
To grin a welcome. So I leave awhile
My hippogriff to crop the magic meads,
And pass into a court the lilies hold,
And tread them to a fragrance that pursues
To win the portico, whose columns, carved
Of lazuli and amber, mock the palms
Of bright Aidennic forests—capitalled
With fronds of stone fretted to airy lace,
Enfolding drupes that seem as tawny clusters
Of breasts of unknown houris; and convolved
With vines of shut and shadowy-leavèd flowers
Like the dropt lids of women that endure

Some loin-dissolving ecstasy. Through doors
Enlaid with lilies twined luxuriously,
I enter, dazed and blinded with the sun,
And hear, in gloom that changing colors cloud,
A chuckle sharp as crepitating ice
Upheaved and cloven by shoulders of the damned
Who strive in Antenora. When my eyes
Undazzle, and the cloud of color fades,
I find me in a monster-guarded room,
Where marble apes with wings of griffins crowd
On walls an evil sculptor wrought; and beasts
Wherein the sloth and vampire-bat unite,
Pendulous by their toes of tarnished bronze,
Usurp the shadowy interval of lamps
That hang from ebon arches. Like a ripple
Borne by the wind from pool to sluggish pool
In fields where wide Cocytus flows his bound,
A crackling smile around that circle runs,
And all the stone-wrought gibbons stare at me
With eyes that turn to glowing coals. A fear
That found no name in Babel, flings me on,
Breathless and faint with horror, to a hall
Within whose weary, self-reverting round,
The languid curtains, heavier than palls,
Unnumerably depict a weary king
Who fain would cool his jewel-crusted hands
In lakes of emerald evening, or the fields
Of dreamless poppies pure with rain. I flee
Onward, and all the shadowy curtains shake
With tremors of a silken-sighing mirth,
And whispers of the innumerable king,
Breathing a tale of ancient pestilence
Whose very words are vile contagion. Then
I reach a room where caryatides,
Carved in the form of voluptuous Titan women,
Surround a throne of flowering ebony
Where creeps a vine of crystal. On the throne
There lolls a wan, enormous Worm, whose bulk,
Tumid with all the rottenness of kings,
Overflows its arms with fold on creasèd fold

Obscenely bloating. Open-mouthed he leans,
And from his fulvous throat a score of tongues,
Depending like to wreaths of torpid vipers,
Drivel with phosphorescent slime, that runs
Down all his length of soft and monstrous folds,
And creeping among the flowers of ebony,
Lends them the life of tiny serpents. Now,
Ere the Horror ope those red and lashless slits
Of eyes that draw the gnat and midge, I turn
And follow down a dusty hall, whose gloom,
Lined by the statues with their mighty limbs,
Ends in a golden-roofèd balcony
Sphering the flowered horizon.

       Ere my heart
Hath hushed the panic tumult of its pulses,
I listen, from beyond the horizon's rim,
A mutter faint as when the far simoon,
Mounting from unknown deserts, opens forth,
Wide as the waste, those wings of torrid night
That shake the doom of cities from their folds,
And musters in its van a thousand winds
That, with disrooted palms for besoms, rise,
And sweep the sands to fury. As the storm,
Approaching, mounts and loudens to the ears
Of them that toil in fields of sesame,
So grows the mutter, and a shadow creeps
Above the gold horizon like a dawn
Of darkness climbing zenith-ward. They come,
The Sabaoth of retribution, drawn
From all dread spheres that knew my trespassing,
And led by vengeful fiends and dire alastors
That owned my sway aforetime! Cockatrice,
Python, tragelaphus, leviathan,
Chimera, martichoras, behemoth,
Geryon, and sphinx, and hydra, on my ken
Arise as might some Afrit-builded city
Consummate in the lifting of a lash
With thunderous domes and sounding obelisks
And towers of night and fire alternate! Wings
Of white-hot stone along the hissing wind

Bear up the huge and furnace-hearted beasts
Of hells beyond Rutilicus; and things
Whose lightless length would mete the gyre of moons—
Born from the caverns of a dying sun—
Uncoil to the very zenith, half-disclosed
From gulfs below the horizon; octopi
Like blazing moons with countless arms of fire,
Climb from the seas of ever-surging flame
That roll and roar through planets unconsumed,
Beating on coasts of unknown metals; beasts
That range the mighty worlds of Alioth rise,
Afforesting the heavens with multitudinous horns
Amid whose maze the winds are lost; and borne
On cliff-like brows of plunging scolopendras,
The shell-wrought towers of ocean-witches loom;
And griffin-mounted gods, and demons throned
On sable dragons, and the cockodrills
That bear the spleenful pygmies on their backs;
And blue-faced wizards from the worlds of Saiph,
On whom Titanic scorpions fawn; and armies
That move with fronts reverted from the foe,
And strike athwart their shoulders at the shapes
Their shields reflect in crystal; and eidola
Fashioned within unfathomable caves
By hands of eyeless peoples; and the blind
Worm-shapen monsters of a sunless world,
With krakens from the ultimate abyss,
And Demogorgons of the outer dark,
Arising, shout with dire multisonous clamors,
And threatening me with dooms ineffable
In words whereat the heavens leap to flame,
Advance upon the enchanted palace. Falling
For league on league before, their shadows blight
And eat like fire the amaranthine meads,
Leaving an ashen desert. In the palace
I hear the apes of marble shriek and howl,
And all the women-shapen columns moan,
Babbling with terror. In my tenfold fear,
A monstrous dread unnamed in any hell,
I rise, and flee with the fleeing wind for wings,

And in a trice the wizard palace reels,
And spiring to a single tower of flame,
Goes out, and leaves nor shard nor ember! Flown
Beyond the world upon that fleeing wind
I reach the gulf's irrespirable verge,
Where fails the strongest storm for breath, and fall,
Supportless, through the nadir-plungèd gloom,
Beyond the scope and vision of the sun,
To other skies and systems.

      In a world
Deep-wooded with the multi-colored fungi
That soar to semblance of fantastic palms,
I fall as falls the meteor-stone, and break
A score of trunks to atom-powder. Unharmed
I rise, and through the illimitable woods,
Among the trees of flimsy opal, roam,
And see their tops that clamber hour by hour
To touch the suns of iris. Things unseen,
Whose charnel breath informs the tideless air
With spreading pools of fetor, follow me,
Elusive past the ever-changing palms;
And pittering moths with wide and ashen wings
Flit on before, and insects ember-hued,
Descending, hurtle through the gorgeous gloom
And quench themselves in crumbling thickets. Heard
Far off, the gong-like roar of beasts unknown
Resounds at measured intervals of time,
Shaking the riper trees to dust, that falls
In clouds of acrid perfume, stifling me
Beneath an irised pall.

       Now the palmettoes
Grow far apart, and lessen momently
To shrubs a dwarf might topple. Over them
I see an empty desert, all ablaze
With amethysts and rubies, and the dust
Of garnets or carnelians. On I roam,
Treading the gorgeous grit, that dazzles me
With leaping waves of endless rutilance,
Whereby the air is turned to a crimson gloom

Through which I wander blind as any Kobold;
Till underfoot the grinding sands give place
To stone or metal, with a massive ring
More welcome to mine ears than golden bells
Or tinkle of silver fountains. When the gloom
Of crimson lifts, I stand upon the edge
Of a broad black plain of adamant that reaches,
Level as windless water, to the verge
Of all the world; and through the sable plain
A hundred streams of shattered marble run,
And streams of broken steel, and streams of bronze,
Like to the ruin of all the wars of time,
To plunge with clangor of timeless cataracts
Adown the gulfs eternal.

    So I follow
Between a river of steel and a river of bronze,
With ripples loud and tuneless as the clash
Of a million lutes; and come to the precipice
From which they fall, and make the mighty sound
Of a million swords that meet a million shields,
Or din of spears and armor in the wars
Of half the worlds and eons. Far beneath
They fall, through gulfs and cycles of the void,
And vanish like a stream of broken stars
Into the nether darkness; nor the gods
Of any sun, nor demons of the gulf,
Will dare to know what everlasting sea
Is fed thereby, and mounts forevermore
In one unebbing tide.

    What nimbus-cloud
Or night of sudden and supreme eclipse,
Is on the suns of opal? At my side
The rivers run with a wan and ghostly gleam
Through darkness falling as the night that falls
From spheres extinguished. Turning, I behold
Betwixt the sable desert and the suns,
The poisèd wings of all the dragon-rout,
Far-flown in black occlusion thousand-fold
Through stars, and deeps, and devastated worlds,

Upon my trail of terror! Griffins, rocs,
And sluggish, dark chimeras, heavy-winged
After the ravin of dispeopled lands,
And harpies, and the vulture-birds of hell,
Hot from abominable feasts, and fain
To cool their beaks and talons in my blood—
All, all have gathered, and the wingless rear,
With rank on rank of foul, colossal Worms,
Makes horrent now the horizon. From the van
I hear the shriek of wyvers, loud and shrill
As tempests in a broken fane, and roar
Of sphinxes, like relentless toll of bells
From towers infernal. Cloud on hellish cloud
They arch the zenith, and a dreadful wind
Falls from them like the wind before the storm,
And in the wind my riven garment streams
And flutters in the face of all the void,
Even as flows a flaffing spirit, lost
On the pit's undying tempest. Louder grows
The thunder of the streams of stone and bronze—
Redoubled with the roar of torrent wings
Inseparably mingled. Scarce I keep
My footing in the gulfward winds of fear,
And mighty thunders beating to the void
In sea-like waves incessant; and would flee
With them, and prove the nadir-founded night
Where fall the streams of ruin. But when I reach
The verge, and seek through sun-defeating gloom
To measure with my gaze the dread descent,
I see a tiny star within the depths—
A light that stays me while the wings of doom
Convene their thickening thousands: for the star
Increases, taking to its hueless orb,
With all the speed of horror-changèd dreams,
The light as of a million million moons;
And floating up through gulfs and glooms eclipsed
It grows and grows, a huge white eyeless Face
That fills the void and fills the universe,
And bloats against the limits of the world
With lips of flame that open. . . .

I. The Star-Treader

The Star-Treader

I

A voice cried to me in a dawn of dreams,
Saying, "Make haste: the webs of death and birth
Are brushed away, and all the threads of earth
Wear to the breaking; spaceward gleams
Thine ancient pathway of the suns,
Whose flame is part of thee;
And the deep gulfs abide coevally
Whose darkness runs
Through all thy spirit's mystery.
Go forth, and tread unharmed the blaze
Of stars wherethrough thou camest in old days;
Pierce without fear each vast
Whose hugeness crushed thee not within the past.
A hand strikes off the chains of Time,
A hand swings back the door of years;
Now fall earth's bonds of gladness and of tears,
And opens the strait dream to space sublime."

II

Who rides a dream, what hand shall stay!
What eye shall note or measure mete
His passage on a purpose fleet,
The thread and weaving of his way!
It caught me from the clasping world,
And swept beyond the brink of Sense,
My soul was flung, and poised, and whirled
Like to a planet chained and hurled
With solar lightning strong and tense.
Swift as communicated rays
That leap from severed suns a gloom

Within whose waste no suns illume,
The wingèd dream fulfilled its ways.
Through years reversed and lit again
I followed that unending chain
Wherein the suns are links of light;
Retraced through lineal, ordered spheres
The twisting of the threads of years
In weavings wrought of noon and night;
Through stars and deeps I watched the dream unroll,
Those folds that form the raiment of the soul.

III

Enkindling dawns of memory,
Each sun had radiance to relume
A sealed, disused, and darkened room
Within the soul's immensity.
Their alien ciphers shown and lit,
I understood what each had writ
Upon my spirit's scroll;
Again I wore mine ancient lives,
And knew the freedom and the gyves
That formed and marked my soul.

IV

I delved in each forgotten mind,
The units that had builded me,
Whose deepnesses before were blind
And formless as infinity—
Knowing again each former world—
From planet unto planet whirled
Through gulfs that mightily divide
Like to an intervital sleep.
One world I found, where souls abide
Like winds that rest upon a rose;
Thereto they creep
To loose all burden of old woes.
And one there was, a garden-close
Whose blooms are grown of ancient sin
And death the sap that wells and flows:
The spirits weep that dwell therein.

And one I knew, where chords of pain
With stridors fill the Senses' lyre;
And one, where Beauty's olden chain
Is forged anew with stranger loveliness,
In flame-soft links of never-quenched desire
And ineluctable duress.

V

Where no terrestrial dreams had trod
My vision entered undismayed,
And Life her hidden realms displayed
To me as to a curious god.
Where colored suns of systems triplicate
Bestow on planets weird, ineffable,
Green light that orbs them like an outer sea,
And large auroral noons that alternate
With skies like sunset held without abate,
Life's touch renewed incomprehensibly
The strains of mirth and grief's harmonious spell.
Dead passions like to stars relit
Shone in the gloom of ways forgot;
Where crownless gods in darkness sit
The day was full on altars hot.
I heard—enisled in those melodic seas—
The central music of the Pleiades,
And to Alcyone my soul
Swayed with the stars that own her song's control.
Unchallenged, glad, I trod, a revenant
In worlds Edenic longly lost;
Or dwelt in spheres that sing to those,
Through space no light has crossed,
Diverse as Hell's mad antiphone uptossed
To Heaven's angelic chant.

VI

What vasts the dream went out to find!
I seemed beyond the world's recall
In gulfs where darkness is a wall
To render strong Antares blind!
In unimagined spheres I found

The sequence of my being's round—
Some life where firstling meed of Song,
The strange imperishable leaf,
Was placed on brows that starry Grief
Had crowned, and Pain anointed long;
Some avatar where Love
Sang like the last great star at morn
Ere the pale orb of Death filled all its sky;
Some life in fresher years unworn
Upon a world whereof
Peace was a robe like to the calms that lie
On pools aglow with latter spring:
There Time's pellucid surface took
Clear image of all things, nor shook
Till the black cleaving of Oblivion's wing;
Some earlier awakening
In pristine years, when giant strife
Of forces darkly whirled
First forged the thing called Life—
Hot from the furnace of the suns—
Upon the anvil of a world.

VII

Thus knew I those anterior ones
Whose lives in mine were blent;
Till, lo! my dream, that held a night
Where Rigel sends no message of his might,
Was emptied of the trodden stars,
And dwindled to the sun's extent—
The brain's familiar prison-bars,
And raiment of the sorrow and the mirth
Wrought by the shuttles intricate of earth.

Ode to the Abyss

O many-gulfed, unalterable one,
Whose deep sustains
Far-drifting world and sun,
Thou wast ere ever star put out on thee;
And thou shalt be

When never world remains;
When all the suns' triumphant strength and pride
Is sunk in voidness absolute,
And their majestic music wide
In vaster silence rendered mute.
And though God's will were night to dusk the blue,
And law to cancel and disperse
The tangled tissues of the universe,
His might were impotent to conquer thee,
O indivisible infinity!
Thy darks subdue
All light that treads thee down a space,
Exulting over thine archetypal deeps.
The cycles die, and lo! thy darkness reaps
The flame of mightiest stars;
In aeon-implicating wars
Thou tearest planets from their place;
Worlds granite-spined
To thine erodents yield
Their treasures centrally confined
In crypts by continental pillars sealed.
What suns and worlds have been thy prey
Through unhorizoned reaches of the past!
What spheres that now essay
Time's undimensioned vast,
Shall plunge forgotten to thy gloom at length
With life that cried its query of the Night
To ears with silence filled!
What worlds unborn shall dare thy strength,
Girt by a sun's unwearied might,
And dip to darkness when the sun is stilled!

O incontestable Abyss,
What light in thine embrace of darkness sleeps—
What blaze of a sidereal multitude
No peopled world is left to miss!
What motion is at rest within thy deeps—
What gyres of planets long become thy food—
Worlds unconstrainable
That plunged therein to peace
Like tempest-worn and crew-forsaken ships;

And suns that fell
To huge and ultimate eclipse,
And from the eternal stances found release!
What sound thy gulfs of silence hold!
Stupendous thunder of the meeting stars
And crash of orbits that diverged,
With Life's thin song are merged;
Thy quietudes enfold
Paean and threnody as one,
And battle-blare of unremembered wars
With festal songs
Sung in the Romes of ruined spheres;
And music that belongs
To undiscoverable younger years
With words of yesterday.
Ah! who may stay
Thy soundless world-devouring tide?
O thou whose hands pluck out the light of stars,
Are worlds but as a destined fruit for thee?
May no sufficient bars
Nor marks inveterate abide
As shores to baffle thine unbillowing sea?
Still and unstriving now,
What plottest thou,
Within thy universe-ulterior deeps,
Dark as the final lull of suns?
What new advancement of the night
On citadels of stars around whose might
Thy slow encroachment runs,
And crouching silence, thunder-potent sleeps?

Nirvana

Poised as a god whose lone, detachèd post,
An eyrie, pends between the boundary-marks
Of finite years and those unvaried darks
That veil Eternity, I saw the host
Of suns and worlds, swept from the furthermost
Of night—confusion as of dust with sparks—
Whirl toward the opposing brink; as one who harks
Some warning trumpet. Time, a withered ghost,

Fled with them: disunited orbs that late
Were atoms of the universal frame,
They passed to some eternal fragment-heap.
And, lo! the gods, from space discorporate,
Who were its life and vital spirit, came,
Drawn voidward by the vampire-lips of Sleep!

The Song of a Comet

Pale plummet of the stark immensities,
From perished heavens cast, I fall and flare
Through gulfs by stellar orbits girdled round;
And spaces bare
Of sparkless night between the galaxies—
By path of sun nor circling planet bound.
No star allots my lone and cyclic gyre;
I mark the systems vanish one by one;
Among the swarming worlds I lunge,
And sudden plunge
Close to the zones of solar fire;
Or 'mid the mighty wrack of stars undone,
Flash, and with momentary rays
Compel the dark to yield
Their aimless forms, whose once far-potent blaze
In ashes chill is now inurned.
Upon the shadowy heavens half-revealed,
I show their planets turned,
Whose strange ephemerae,
On adamantine tablets deeply written,
In cities long unlitten,
Have left their history
And lore beyond redemption or surmise.
Adown contiguous skies,
I pass the thickening brume
Of systems yet unshaped, that hang immense
Along mysterious shores of gloom;
Or see—unimplicated in their doom—
The final and disastrous gyre
Of blinded suns that meet,
And from their mingled heat

And battle-clouds intense,
Overspread the deep with fire.

Upon the Lion's track,
Or far beyond the abysms of the Lyre,
I thread, through mazes of the zodiac,
Mine orbit placed amid
The multiple and irised stars, or hid,
Unsolved and intricate,
In many a planet-swinging sun's estate.
At times I steal in solitary flight
Along the rim of the exterior night
That rounds the universe;
And then return,
Past outer footholds of sidereal light,
To see the systems gather and disperse;
And learn
What vast and multifarious marvels wait
In the dim void that has no ultimate;
What wraiths of suns extinguished long ago
On alien welkins burn;
What flaming blossoms grow
From the black battlefields of cosmic wars;
What stellar hells, or ampler spheres sublime,
Enisled in diverse time,
Are wrought from sharded moons and meteors;
And haply I discern
What paler fires, to mine own self akin,
Still haunt the night's eternal corridors,
Or in the toils of great Arcturus spin.
Then, restless still, I rise
Through vaults of mightier gloom, to watch the dark
Snatch at the flame of failing suns;
Or mark
That midden of the stagnant nadir skies
Where many a fated orbit runs.
An arrow sped from some forgotten bow,
Through change of firmaments and systems sent,
And finding bourn nor bars,
I fly, nor know
For what remoter mark my flight is meant.

Lament of the Stars

One tone is mute within the starry singing,
The unison fulfilled, complete before;
One chord within the music sounds no more,
And from the stir of flames forever winging
The pinions of our sister, motionless
In pits of indefinable duress,
Are fallen beyond all recovery
By exultation of the flying dance,
Or rhythms holding as with sleep or trance
The maze of stars that only death may free—
Flung through the void's expanse.

In gulfs depressed nor in the gulfs exalted
Shall shade nor lightening of her flame be found;
In space that litten orbits gird around,
Nor in the bottomless abyss unvaulted
Of unenvironed, all-outlying night.
Allotted gyre nor lawless comet-flight
Shall find, and with its venturous ray return
From gloom of undiscoverable scope,
One ray of her to gladden into hope
The doubtful eyes denied that truthward yearn,
The faltering feet that grope.

Beyond restrainless boundary-nights surpassing
All luminous horizons limited,
The substance and the light of her have fed
Ruin and silence of the night's amassing:
Abandoned worlds forever morningless;
Suns without worlds, in frory beamlessness
Girt for the longer gyre funereal;
Inviolate silence, earless, unawaking
That once was sound, and level calm unbreaking
Where motion's many ways in oneness fall
Of sleep beyond forsaking.

Circled with limitation unexceeded
Our eyes behold exterior mysteries
And gods unascertainable as these—
Shadows and shapes irresolubly heeded;

Phantoms that tower, and substance scarcely known.
Our sister knows all mysteries one alone,
One shape, one shadow, crowding out the skies;
Whose eyeless head and lipless face debar
All others nameless or familiar,
Filling with night all former lips and eyes
Of god, and ghost, and star:

For her all shapes have fed the shape of night;
All darker forms, and dubious forms, or pallid,
Are met and reconciled where none is valid.
But unto us solution nor respite
Of mystery's multiform incessancy
From unexplored or system-trodden sky
Shall come; but as a load importunate,
Enigma past and mystery foreseen
Weigh mightily upon us, and between
Our sorrow deepens, and our songs abate
In cadences of threne.

A gloom that gathers silence looms more closely,
And quiet centering darkness at its heart;
But from the certitude of night depart
Uncertain god nor eidolon less ghostly;
But stronger grown with strength obtained from light
That failed, and power lent by the stronger night,
Perplex us with new mystery, and doubt
If these our flames, that deathward toss and fall
Be festal lights or lights funereal
For mightier gods within the gulfs without,
Phantoms more cryptical.

New shadows from the wings of Time unfolding
Across the depth and eminence of years,
Fall deeplier with the broadening gloom of fears.
Prophetic-eyed, with planet-hosts beholding
The night take form upon the face of suns,
We see (thus grief's vaticination runs—
Presageful sorrow for our sister slain)
A night wherein all sorrow shall be past,
One with night's single mystery at last;

Nor vocal sun nor singing world remain
As Time's elegiast.

In Saturn

Upon the seas of Saturn I have sailed
To isles of high primeval amarant,
Where the flame-tongued, sonorous flowers enchant
The hanging surf to silence; all engrailed

With ruby-colored pearls, the golden shore
Allured me; but as one whom spells restrain,
For blind horizons of the somber main
And harbors never known, my singing prore

I set forthrightly. Formed of fire and brass,
And arched with moons, immenser heavens deep
Were opened—till above the darkling foam,

With dome on cloudless adamantine dome,
Black peaks no peering seraph deems to pass
Rose up from realms ineffable as sleep!

Triple Aspect

Lo, for Earth's manifest monotony
Of ordered aspect unto sun and star,
And single moon, I turn to years afar
And ampler worlds ensphered in memory.

There, to the zoned and iris-varying light
Of three swift suns in heavens of vaster range,
Transcendent beauty knows a trinal change,
And dawn and eve are in the place of night.

There, long ago, in mornings ocean-green,
I saw vast deserts verdant with the sky,
Or under yellow noons wide waters lie
Like molten bronze that boiled with fires unseen.

Strange flowers that bloom but to an azure sun
I saw; and all complexities of light

That work fantastic magic on the sight
Wrought unimagined marvels one by one.

There, swifter shadows suffer gorgeous dooms—
Lost in an orange noon, an azure morn;
At twofold eve large, wingèd lights are born,
Towering to meet the dawn, or briefest glooms

Of chrysoberyl filled with alien stars
Draw from an emerald east to skies of gold.
Toward jasper waters leaning to behold,
Vague moons are lost amid great nenuphars.

The Abyss Triumphant

The force of suns had waned beyond recall.
Chaos was re-established over all,
Where lifeless atoms through forgetful deeps
Fled unrelated, cold, immusical.

Above the tumult heaven alone endured;
Long since the bursting walls of hell had poured
Demon and damned to peace erstwhile denied,
Within the Abyss God's might had not immured.

(He could but thwart it with creative mace. . . .)
And now it rose about the heavenly base,
Mordant at pillars rotten through and through
Of Matter's last, most firm abiding-place.

Bastion and minaret began to nod,
Till all the pile, unmindful of His rod,
Dissolved in thunder, and the void Abyss
Caught like a quicksand at the feet of God!

The Motes

I saw a universe today:
Through a disclosing bar of light
The motes were whirled in gleaming flight
That briefly dawned and sank away.

Each had its swift and tiny noon;
In orbit-streams I marked them flit,
Successively revealed and lit.
The sunlight paled and shifted soon.

Desire of Vastness

Supreme with night, what high mysteriarch—
The undreamt-of god beyond the trinal noon
Of elder suns empyreal—past the moon
Circling some wild world outmost in the dark—
Lays on me this unfathomed wish to hark
What central sea with plume-plucked midnight strewn,
Plangent to what enormous plenilune
That lifts in silence, hinderless and stark?

The brazen empire of the bournless waste,
The unstayed dominions of the brazen sky—
These I desire, and all things wide and deep;
And, lifted past the level years, would taste
The cup of an Olympian ecstasy,
Titanic dream, and Cyclopean sleep.

Shadows

Thy shadow falls on the fount,
On the fount with the marble wall. . . .
And in alien time and space
On the towns of a doomèd race
The shadows of glaciers mount;
And patchouli-shadows crawl
On the mottling of boas that bask
In the fire of a moon fantasque;
And the light shades of bamboo
Flutter and ruffle and lift,
In the silver dawn they sift
On the meadows of Xanadu. . . .
They shall fall, till the light be done,
By moon and cresset and sun,
From gnomon and fir-tree and throne,

And the vine-caught monoliths leaning
In the woods of a world far-flown;
They shall pass on the dim star-dials
By the peoples of Pluto wrought;
They shall follow the shifted vials
Of a sorceress of Fomalhaut;
They shall move on the primal plains
In the broken thunder and rains;
They shall haply reel and soar
Where the red volcanoes roar
From the peaks of a blackening sun;
They shall haply float and run
From the tails of the lyre-birds preening
On the palms of a magic mead;
And their mystery none shall read,
And none shall have known their meaning
Ere night and the shadows are one.

A Dream of the Abyss

I seemed at the sheer end:
Albeit mine eyes, in mystery and night
Shrouded as with the close deep caul of death,
Or as if underneath Lethean lentors drowned,
Saw never lamp nor star nor dead star's wraith of light,
Yet seemed I at the world's sheer end;
And fearfully and slowly I drew breath
From silent gulfs of all uncertainty and dread,
Precipitate to nadir from around;
Nor trusted I on any side to tread
One pace, lest I should overstep the brink,
And infinitely and forever sink
Past eye-shot of the Cyclopean sun
When from the bulwark of the world, adown oblivion,
He on the morrow should stare after me.

Swift from infinity,
The enormous Fear that lives between the stars
Clutched with the cold great darkness at my heart;
Then from the gulf arose a whispering,

And rustle as of silence on the wing
To stay and stand
Anear at my right hand:
What powers abysmal, born of the blind air,
What nameless demons of the nether deep
That 'scape the sun and from the moonlight live apart,
Came and conspired against me there,
I heard not, ere the whispering
Ceased, and a heavier darkness seemed to spring
Upon me, and I felt the silence leap
And clasp me closer, and the sweep
Of all the abyss reach up and drag
Body and feet from the crumbling uttermost crag
To the emptiness unknown;
Nor knew I, plunging through those nadir firmaments,
If Azrael or Abbadon bore me thence,
Or if I fell alone.

After Armageddon

God walks lightly in the gardens of a cold, dark star,
Knowing not the dust that gathers in His garments' fold;
God signs Him with the clay, marks Him with the mould,
Walking in the fields unsunned of a sad, lost war,
In a star long cold.

God treads brightly where the bones of unknown things lie,
Pale with His splendor as the frost in a moon-bleached place;
God sees the tombs by the light of His face,
He shudders at the runes writ thereon, and His shadow on the sky
Shudders hugely in space.

God talks briefly with His armies of the tomb-born worm,
God holds parley with the grey worm and pale, avid moth:
Their mouths have eaten all, but the worm is wroth
With a dark hunger still, and he murmurs harm
With the murmuring moth.

God turns Him heavenward in haste from a death-dark star,
But His robes are assoilèd by the dust of unknown things dead;
The grey worm follows creeping, and the pale moth has fed

Couched in a secret golden fold of His broad-trained cimar
Like a doom unsaid.

The Ancient Quest

O giant stars, born of eternal night,
O wingèd flames wherewith the void is sown,
As dreadful prophets of a God unknown,
Ye speak the law in light!

Had we but sight to see and comprehend,
Your countless fires were as a language plain
To tell us all that we have sought in vain;
The quest were at an end.

O younger worlds, whose tireless-pinioned flight
Climbs eagerly the sheer and topless deep!
O shrivelled planets that obscurely creep
On orbits sunk in night!

Alike ye falter in unceasing gloom
That shrouds the deathless Truth ye may not find;
Alike for ye the flaming suns are blind,
And light may not illume.

For Life whose God-ambitious eyes would see
The stellar-manifested truth sublime,
Must gaze with sight immutable as Time,
Large as Infinity.

A Dream of Oblivion

The day of Time was darkening to its end:
The sun hung chill within the blackened noon,
Its splendours one with night. From planets doomed
The wail of death to empty silence rose.
The stars were faint against the glooming vast,
Like wavering lights upon a windy plain
That one by one go out; and even as these,
The eternal suns expired, and left a void—
A huge and black Nirvana of the skies—

A visible Oblivion. Then came down
The darkness and the silence on all things,
The worlds that eddy like wind-driven leaves
Within the airless deep, and souls of men,
And on all Life. The universe was night,
And this strange, troubled dream of Time and Place
A still vacuity. These things I knew,
When, lo! beneath my feet the steadfast earth
Grew nothingness, and down the gulf I fell,
And with the darkness and the silence merged.

Ode to Light

What sky beheld thy primal birth,
When ageless night's dimensionless extent
First knew division, and the girth
Of formless heavens constraint and measurement;
And when thy touch was laid
On chaos, till its atom-surge
Subsided as the breast
Of ocean, when above the night's unrest
The morning leaps, arrayed
In vesture of unshadowed skies?
Was it in any deep our sight descries,
Or past the verge
Of vision in a firmament withheld,
That, like a flower from the primordial dust,
Thy sun original upsprang—
Lone, ere the constellations sang
Their youthful paean unexcelled,
Bright in the first completion of their choir—
Their fulness ere the hand of Death outthrust
Broke that continuousness of younger fire?
Burns yet thine earliest star?
Or sank its flame
Ere came
Aldebaran and Algebar;
Or stout Orion rose, fulfilled
With all his starry frame?
Ere any world that now

Treads to a sun unchilled,
Might look upon its flaming brow,
Or note its fall from paths of light uplifted,
To where, within the irremeable pit,
All suns dethroned have drifted
To sunken paths unlit?
Have all its brethren found that place,
Where iron-relentless shadows hem,
Seeing the ruinous maw
As when the falling Titans saw
The gulf of Tartarus opening under them
Like visible oblivion, for the space
Ere they were one with it?

Ode to Matter

O tissued fabric of the frame of things,
Thou art an alternating tide,
And Life a moment's foam
Thy shifting wave upflings.
Billowed with suns and worlds that roam
Where winds of Force direct with driving wings,
Thy depths immingle and divide—
A sea whereto the gulfs as shores abide.
In peaceless rounds of change,
Thy forms irrevocably flee:
Inevitable laws estrange
All shapes of stars and worlds that be,
And like a mist's inconstant fantasy,
Ensphered anew, as alien forms they range.
Lo! here a sun is smitten into night—
One with the cosmic mire;
And yonder startles into fire
The dust of stars destroyed,
Whose quickened worlds resume their ancient flight,
Till arms of darkness, rising from the void,
Drag down the pillared suns again;
And other systems rise and wane,
Rebuilt from star and asteroid.

Lo! is there end
Or rest unto thy toil—
Thou who createst many forms,
Yet none that stay, of all thy fruitful soil?
Shall all the terms of living suns extend
And find thy labour incomplete?
All storms
Where stars irreparably meet
Prepare not thy potential field
Unto some larger yield
Than aught the systems show—some fruit more great—
Some flower ultimate?
Thine atoms pour
Through moulds of many worlds and suns,
As they have passed
In years beyond all memory and lore;
As they shall flee while Time his orbit runs,
Along abysmal aeons cast.

What strivest thou to build
With dust of systems reared and rent
And flame of suns blown out and lit again?
Dost toil with hands as yet unskilled
To some obscurely known intent,
Far-sought through mists of weariness and pain?
Ah, dare we dream
That thou shalt dream no fairer thing than man,
No higher world than this?
That from thine unexplorable abyss
No stronger Life shall rise supreme,
Wrought from rejected dust whereof began
All former Life—
The dust remoulded through abyssal strife
Within the suns' uncompassable scheme?

II. Medusa and Other Horrors

Nero

This Rome, that was the toil of many men,
The consummation of laborious years—
Fulfillment's crown to visions of the dead
And image of the wide desire of kings—
Is made my darkling dream's effulgency,
Fuel of vision, brief embodiment
Of wandering will and wastage of the strong
Fierce ecstasy of one tremendous hour,
When ages piled on ages like a pyre
Flamed to the years behind and years to be.

Yet any sunset were as much as this,
Save for the music forced from tongueless things,
The rape of Matter's huge, unchorded harp
By the many-fingered fire—a music pierced
With the tense voice of Life, more quick to cry
Its agony—and save that I believed
The radiance redder for the blood of men.
Destruction hastens and intensifies
The process that is beauty, manifests
Ranges of form unknown before, and gives
Motion, and voice, and hue, where otherwise
Bleak inexpressiveness had levelled all.

If one create, there is the lengthy toil;
The labored years and days league toward an end
Less than the measure of desire, mayhap,
After the sure consuming of all strength
And strain of faculties that otherwhere
Were loosed upon enjoyment; and at last
Remains to one capacity nor power

For pleasure in the thing that he hath made.
But on destruction hangs but little use
Of time or faculty, but all is turned
To the one purpose, unobstructed, pure,
Of sensuous rapture and observant joy;
And from the intensities of death and ruin
One draws a heightened and completer life,
And both extends and vindicates himself.

I would I were a god, with all the scope
Of attributes that are the essential core
Of godhead, and its visibility.
I am but emperor, and hold awhile
The power to hasten death upon its way,
And cry a halt to worn and lagging Life
For others, but for mine own self may not
Delay the one nor bid the other speed.
There have been many kings, and they are dead,
And have no power in death save what the wind
Confers upon their blown and brainless dust
To vex the eyeballs of posterity.
But were I God, I would be overlord
Of many kings, and were as breath to guide
Their dust of destiny. And were I God,
Exempt from this mortality which clogs
Perception and clear exercise of will,
What rapture it would be, if but to watch
Destruction crouching at the back of Time,
The tongueless dooms which dog the travelling suns;
The vampire, Silence, at the breast of worlds,
Fire without light that gnaws the base of things,
And Lethe's mounting tide that rots the stone
Of fundamental spheres. This were enough
Till such time as the dazzled wings of will
Came up with power's accession, scarcely felt
For very suddenness. Then I would urge
The strong contention and conflicting might
Of Chaos and Creation—matching them,
Those immemorial powers inimical,
And all their stars and gulfs subservient,
Dynasts of time, and anarchs of the dark—

In closer war reverseless, and would set
New discord at the universal core—
A Samson-principle to bring it down
In one magnificence of ruin. Yea,
The monster, Chaos, were mine unleashed hound,
And all my power Destruction's own right arm!

I would exult to mark the smouldering stars
Renew beneath my breath their elder fire
And feed upon themselves to nothingness.
The might of suns—slow-paced with swinging weight
Of myriad worlds—were made at my desire
One orb of roaring and torrential light,
Through which the voice of Life were audible,
And singing of the immemorial dead,
Whose dust is loosened into vaporous wings
With soaring wrack of systems ruinous.
And were I weary of the glare of these,
I would tear out the eyes of light, and stand
Above a chaos of extinguished suns,
That crowd and grind and shiver thunderously,
Lending vast voice and motion by no ray
To the stretched silence of the blinded gulfs.
Thus would I give my godhead space and speech
For its assertion, and thus pleasure it,
Hastening the feet of Time with cast of worlds
Like careless pebbles, or, with shattered suns,
Brightening the aspect of Eternity.

Medusa

As drear and barren as the glooms of Death,
It lies, a windless land of livid dawns,
Nude to a desolate firmament, with hills
That seem the gibbous bones of the mummied Earth,
And plains whose hollow face is rivelled deep
With gullies twisting like a serpent's track.
The leprous touch of Death is on its stones,
Where, for his token visible, the Head
Is throned upon a heap of monstrous rocks
Rough-mounded like some shattered pyramid

In a thwartly cloven hill-ravine, that seems
The unhealing scar of huge Tellurian wars.
Her lethal beauty crowned with twining snakes
That mingle with her hair, the Gorgon reigns.
Her eyes are clouds wherein black lightnings lurk,
Yet, even as men that seek the glance of Life,
The gazers come, where, coiled and serpent-swift,
Those levins wait. As round an altar-base
Her victims lie, distorted, blackened forms
Of postured horror smitten into stone—
Time caught in meshes of Eternity—
Drawn back from dust and ruin of the years,
And given to all the future of the world.
The land is claimed of Death: the daylight comes
Half-strangled in the changing webs of cloud
That unseen spiders of bewildered winds
Weave and unweave across the lurid sun
In upper air. Below, no zephyr comes
To break with life the circling spell of doom.
Long vapor-serpents twist about the moon,
And in the windy murkness of the sky
The guttering stars are wild as candle-flames
That near the socket.

     Thus the land shall be,
And Death shall wait, throned in Medusa's eyes,
Till in the irremeable webs of night
The sun is snared, and the corroded moon
A dust upon the gulfs, and all the stars
Rotted and fallen like rivets from the sky,
Letting the darkness down upon all things.

Averted Malefice

Where mandrakes, crying from the moonless fen,
Told how a witch, with eyes of owl or bat,
Found, and each root maleficently fat
Pulled for her waiting cauldron, on my ken
Upstole, escaping to the world of men,
A vapor as of some infernal vat;

Across the stars it clomb, and caught thereat
As if their bright regard to veil again.

Despite the web, methought they knew, appalled,
The stealthier weft in which all sound was still. . . .
Then sprang, as if the night found breath anew,
A wind whereby the stars were disenthralled. . . .
Far off, I heard the cry of frustrate ill,
A witch that wailed above her curdled brew.

The Medusa of the Skies

Like a worm-fretted visage from the tomb,
The moon unswathes her hollow, shrunken head,
Launching such light as foulders on the dead
From pallid skies more death-like than the gloom.
Under her beams the breasted lands assume
Dead hues, and charnel shapes uncerememented;
And shadows that towering sepulchers might shed
More livid as the shadows on dials of doom.

On hills like tumuli, and waters mute,
A whiteness steals as of a world made still
When reptant Death at last rears absolute—
An earth now frozen by malefice of eyes
Aeonian dooms and realm-deep rigors fill—
The gaze of that Medusa of the skies.

Saturn

Now were the Titans gathered round their king
In a waste region slipping toward the verge
Of drear extremities that clasp the world—
A land half-moulded by the hasty gods,
Grotesque, misfeatured, blackly gnarled with stone,
And left beneath the bright scorn of the stars;
Or worn and marred from conflict with the deep,
Conterminate, of Chaos. Here they stood,
Old Saturn midmost, like a central peak
Among the lesser mounts that guard its base.
Defeat, that gloamed within each countenance

Like the first tinge of death, upon a sun
Gathering like some dusk vapor, found them cold,
Heavy of limb, and halting as with weight
Of threatened worlds and trembling firmaments.
A wind cried round them like a trumpet-voice
Of phantom hosts—hurried, importunate,
And intermittent with a tightening fear.
Far off the sunset sprang, and the hard clouds,
Molten among the peaks, seemed furnaces
In which to make the fetters of the world.

Seared by the lightning of the younger gods,
They saw, beyond the grim and crouching hills,
Those levins thrust like spears into the heart
Of swollen clouds, or cleaving the dark sky
Like swords colossal. Then, as the Titans watched,
The night rose like a black, enormous mist
Around them wherein naught was visible
Save the sharp levin leaping in the north;
And no sound came except of seas remote
That seemed like Chaos ravening past the verge
Of all the world, fed with the crumbling coasts
Of Matter.

   Till the moon, discovering
That harsh swart wilderness of sand and stone
Tissued and twisted in chaotic weld,
Lit with illusory fire each Titan's form,
They sate in silence, mute as stranded orbs—
The wrack of Time, upcast on ruinous coasts,
And in the slow withdrawal of the tide
Unvexed awhile. Small solace could they take
From that wan radiance glistering frostily
Upon the desert seized in iron silence,
Like a false triumph over contestless Fates,
Or a mirage of life in wastes of death.
Yet were they moved to speak, and Saturn's voice,
Seeming the soul of that tremendous land
Set free in sound, startled the haughty stars:

"O Titans, gods, sustainers of the world,
 Is this the end? Must Earth go down to Chaos,

Lacking our strength, beneath the unpractised sway
Of godlings vain, precipitate with youth,
Who think, unrecking of disastrous chance,
To bind their will as reins upon the sun,
Or stand as columns to the ponderous heavens?
Must we behold with eyes of impotence
That universal wrack, even though it whelm
These our usurpers in impartial doom
Beneath the shards and fragments of the world?
Were it not preferable to return,
And, meeting them in fight unswervable,
Drag down the earth, ourselves, and these our foes,
One sacrifice unto the gods of Chaos?
Why should we stay, and live the tragedy
Of power that survives its use?"

                            Now spake
Enceladus, when that the echoings
Of Saturn's voice had fled remote, and seemed
Dead thunders caught and flung from star to star:
"Wouldst hurl thy kingdom down the nightward gulf
Like to a stone a curious child might cast
To test the fall of some dark precipice?
Patience and caution should we take as mail,
Not rashness for a weapon—too keen sword
That cuts the strainèd knot of destiny,
Never to be tied again. Were it not best
To watch the slow procedure of the days,
That we may grasp a time more opportune
When desperation is not all our strength
Nor the foe newly filled with victory?
Then may we hope to conquer back thy realm
For thee, not for the gods of nothingness?"

He ceased, and after him no lesser god
Gave voice upon the shaken silences,
None venturing to risk comparison,
Inevitable then, of eloquence
With his; but, like the ambiguity
Of signal stars and lesser overcast
And merged in one confusion by the moon,

Silence possessed that throng, till Saturn rose.
Around his form the light intensified,
And strengthened with addition wild and strange,
Investing him as with a ghostly robe
And gathering like a crown about his brow.
His sword, whereon the shadows lay like rust,
He took, and dipping it within the moon
Made clean its length of blade and from it cast
Swift flickerings at the stars. And then his voice
Came like a torrent, and from out his eyes
Streamed wilder power that mingled with the sound.

And his resurgent power, in glance and word,
Poured through the Titans' souls and was become
The fountains of their own, and at his flame
Their fires relumined twice-rebellious rose,
Leaping against the stronghold of the stars.
And now they turned, majestic with resolve,
Where, red upon the forefront of the north,
Arcturus was a beacon to the winds.
And with the flickering winds, that lightly struck
The desert dust, then sprang again in air,
They passed athwart the foreland of the north,
Against their march they saw the shrunken waste,
A rivelled region like a world grown old
Whose sterile breast knew not the lips of life
In all its epoch; or a world that was
The nurse of infant Death, ere he became
Too large, too strong for its restraining arms,
And towered athwart the suns.

                                          And there they crossed
Metallic slopes that rang like monstrous shields
Under their tread, and dully clanging plains
Like body-mail of greater, vaster gods.
Where hills made gibbous shadows in the moon,
They heard the eldritch laughters of the wind,
Seeming the mirth of doom; and 'neath their gaze
Gaunt valleys deepened like an old despair.
Yet strode they on through the moon's fantasies,
Bold with resolve, across a land like doubt.

And now they passed among huge mountain-bulks,
Themselves like ambulant mountains, moving slow
'Mid fettered brethren, adding weight and gloom
To that mute conclave great against the stars.
Emerging thence the Titans marched where still
Their own portentous shadows went before
Like night that fled but shrunk not, dusking all
That desert way.
              And now they came where sleep,
The sleep of weary victory, had seized
The younger gods as captives, borne beyond
All flight of mounting battle-ecstasies
In that deep triumph of forgetfulness.
Upon that sleep the striding Titans broke,
Vague and immense at first like forming dreams
To those disturbèd gods, in mist of drowse
Purblind and doubtful yet, though soon they knew
Their erst-defeated foes, and rising stood
In silent ranks expectant, that appeared
To move, with shaking of astonished fires
That bristled forth deployed like awful plumes
Between the brightening desert and the sky.
Then, sudden as the waking from a dream,
The battle sprang, where striving deities
Moved brightly through the whirled and stricken air,
Sweeping it to a froth of fire; and all
That ancient, deep-established desert rocked,
Shaken as by an onset of the gulfs
Of gathered and impatient Chaos, while,
Above the place where central battle burned,
The moon and stars drew back in dazzlement,
Paling to more secluded distances.
Lo, where the moon's uncertain light had wrought
Disordered shadows and chimeras dim,
Hiding the hideous desert with mirage,
Or deepening it with gulfs and glooms of hell,
Mightier confusion, chaos absolute,
Was grown the one thing sure in sky or world.
Typhonian maelstroms caught in fiery storms,
Torn by the sweep of Olympian weaponries—

Crescented blades that met with rounds of shields;
Grappling of shapes, seen through the riven blaze
An instant, then once more obscure and known
Only by giant heavings of that war
Of furious gods and rousèd elements—
These, round one swollen center, hung ensphered
Upon the blasted sand and molten rocks.

So huge that chaos, complicate within
With movements of gigantic legionry,
Where Jove and Saturn, thunder-crested, led
In onset never stayed—so strong the strife
Of differing impulse, that decision found
No foothold, till that first confusion should
In ordered conflict re-arrange and stand
With its true forces known. This seemed remote
With that wide struggle pending terribly,
As if the spectrumed wings of Time had made
A truce with white Eternity, and both
Stood watching from afar.

                        Through drifts of haze
The broadening moon, made ominous with red,
Glared from the westering night. And now that war
Built for itself, far up, a cope of cloud
And drew it down, far off, upon all sides,
Impervious to the moon and sworded stars.
And by their own wild light the gods fought on
'Neath that stupendous concave like a sky
Filled and illumined with glare of shattered suns.
And cast by their own light, upon that sky
The gods' own shadows moved like shapen gloom,
Phantasmagoric, changed and amplified,
A shifting frieze that flickered dreadfully
In spectral battle indecisive. Then,
Swift as it had begun, the contest turned
And on the heaving Titans' massive front
It seemed that all the motion and the strength
Self-thwarting and confounded, of that strife,
Was flung in centered impact terrible,
With rush of all that fire, tempestuous-blown

As if before some wind of further space
Striking the earth. Lo, all the Titans' flame
Bent back upon themselves and they were hurled
In vaster disarray, with vanguard piled
On rear and center. Saturn could not stem
The loosened torrents of long-pent defeat;
He, with his hosts, was but as drift thereon,
Borne wildly down the whelmed and reeling world.

Hurling like slanted rain, the violet levin
Fell over the flight of Titans, and behind,
In striding menace, all-victorious Jove
Loomed like some craggy cloud with thunders crowned
And footed with the winds. In that defeat,
With Jove's pursuit deepened and manifold,
Few found escape unscathed, and some went down
Like senile suns that grapple with the dark,
And reel in flame tremendous, and are still.

Ebbing, the battle left those elder gods
Thrown back on iron shores of their despair,
A darker and a vaster Tartarus.
The victor gods, their storms and thunders spent,
Went dwindling northward like embattled clouds,
And, where the lingering haze of fight dissolved,
The pallor of the dawn began to spread
On darkness purple like the pain of death.
Ringed with that desolation Saturn stood
Mute, and the Titans answered unto him
With brother silence. Motionless, they appeared
Some peristyle of topless columns great,
Alone enduring of a fallen fane
In wastes of an immenser world whence Life
And Faith have vanished, whose enshadowed orb
Verges oblivionward. And Twilight slow
Crept round those lofty shapes august and seemed
Such as might be the ghostly, muffled noon
Of mightier suns that totter down to death.

Then turned they, passing from that dismal place
Blasted anew with battle, ere the dawn,
Striding in flame athwart stupendous chasms

And wasteful plains, should overtake them there,
Bowed with too heavy a burden of defeat.
Slowly they turned, and passed upon the west
Where, like a weariness immovable
In menace huge, the plain its monstrous bulk,
The peaks its hydra heads, the whole world crouched
Against their march with the diminished stars.

In Lemuria

Rememberest thou? Enormous gongs of stone
Were stricken, and the storming trumpeteers
Acclaimed my deed to answering tides of spears,
And spoke the names of monsters overthrown—
Griffins whose angry gold, and fervid store
Of sapphires wrenched from mountain-plungèd mines—
Carnelians, opals, agates, almandines,
I brought to thee some scarlet eve of yore.

In the wide fane that shrined thee Venus-wise,
The fallen clamors died. . . . I heard the tune
Of tiny bells of pearl and melanite,
Hung at thy knees, and arms of dreamt delight;
And placed my wealth before thy fabled eyes,
Pallid and pure as jaspers from the moon.

Satan Unrepentant

Lost from those archangelic thrones that star,
Fadeless and fixed, heaven's light of azure bliss;
Forbanned of all His splendor and depressed
Beyond the birth of the first sun, and lower
Than the last star's decline, I still endure,
Abased, majestic, fallen, beautiful,
And unregretful in the doubted dark,
Throneless, that greatens chaos-ward, albeit
From chanting stars that throng the nave of night
Lost echoes wander here, and of His praise
With ringing moons for cymbals dinned afar,
And shouted from the flaming mouths of suns.

The shadows of impalpable blank deeps—
Deep upon deep accumulate—close down,
Around my head concentered, while above,
In the lit, loftier blue, star after star
Spins endless orbits betwixt me and heaven;
And at my feet mysterious Chaos breaks,
Abrupt, immeasurable. Round His throne
Throbs now the rhythmic resonance of suns,
Incessant, perfect, music infinite:
I, throneless, hear the discords of the dark,
And roar of ruin uncreate, than which
Some vast cacophony of dragons, heard
In wasted worlds, were purer melody.

The universe His tyranny constrains
Turns on: in old and consummated gulfs
The stars that wield His judgement wait at hand,
And in new deeps Apocalyptic suns
Prepare His coming: lo, His mighty whim
To rear and mar, goes forth enormously
In nights and constellations! Darkness hears
Enragèd suns that bellow down the deep
God's ravenous and insatiable will;
And He is strong with change, and rideth forth
In whirlwind clothed, with thunders and with doom
To the red stars: God's throne is reared of change;
Its myriad and successive hands support
Like music His omnipotence, that fails
If mercy or if justice interrupt
The sequence of that tyranny, begun
Upon injustice, and doomed evermore
To stand thereby.

I, who with will not less
Than His, but lesser strength, opposed to Him
This unsubmissive brow and lifted mind,
He holds remote in nullity and night
Doubtful between old Chaos and the deeps
Betrayed by Time to vassalage. Methinks
All tyrants fear whom they may not destroy,
And I, that am of essence one with His,

Though less in measure, He may not destroy,
And but withstands in gulfs of dark suspense,
A secret dread for ever: for God knows
This quiet will irrevocably set
Against His own, and this my prime revolt
Yet stubborn, and confirmed eternally.
And with the hatred born of fear, and fed
Ever thereby, God hates me, and His gaze
Sees the bright menace of mine eyes afar
Through midnight, and the innumerable blaze
Of servile suns: lo, strong in tyranny,
The despot trembles that I stand opposed!
For fain am I to hush the anguished cries
Of Substance, broken on the racks of change,
Of Matter tortured into life; and God,
Knowing this, dreads evermore some huge mishap—
That in the vigils of Omnipotence,
Once careless, I shall enter heaven, or He,
Himself, with weight of some unwonted act,
Thoughtless perturb His balanced tyranny,
To mine advance of watchful aspiration.

With rumored thunder and enormous groan
(Burden of sound that heavens overborne
Let slip from deep to deep, even to this
Where climb the huge cacophonies of Chaos)
God's universe moves on. Confirmed in pride,
In patient majesty serene and strong,
I wait the dreamt, inevitable hour
Fulfilled of orbits ultimate, when God,
Whether through His mischance or mine own deed,
Or rise of other and extremer Strength,
Shall vanish, and the lightened universe
No more remember Him than Silence does
An ancient thunder. I know not if these,
Mine all-indomitable eyes, shall see
A maimed and dwindled Godhead cast among
The stars of His creating, and beneath
The unnumbered rush of swift and shining feet
Trodden into night; or mark the fiery breath
Of His infuriate suns blaze forth upon

And scorch that coarsened Essence; or His flame,
A mightier comet, roar and redden down,
Portentous unto Chaos. I but wait,
In strong majestic patience equable,
That hour of consummation and of doom,
Of justice, and rebellion justified.

The Ghoul and the Seraph

Scene: A cemetery by moonlight. The Ghoul emerges from the shade of a cypress and sings.

THE SONG

The Pestilence is on the wing!
Behold! the sweet and crimson foam
Upon the lips of churl and king!
No worm but hath a feastful home:
The Pestilence is on the wing!

Even now his kiss incarnadines
The brows of maiden, queen and whore;
The nun to him her cheek resigns;
Wan lips were never kissed before,
His ancient kiss incarnadines.

Good cheer to thee, white worm of death!
The priest within the brothel dies,
The bawd hath sickened from his breath!
In grave half-dug the digger lies:
Good cheer to thee, white worm of death!

(The Seraph appears from among the trees, half walking, half flying, with wings whose iris the moonlight has rendered faint, and pauses at sight of the Ghoul.)

THE SERAPH

What gardener in crudded fields of hell,
Or scullion of the Devil's house, art thou—
To whom the filth of Malebolge clings,
 And reek of horrid refuse? Thou art gnurled
And black as any Kobold from the mines

Where demons delve for orichalch and steel
To forge the infernal racks! Upon thy face,
Detestable and evil as might haunt
The last delirium of a dying hag,
Or necromancer's madness, fall thy locks
Like sodden reeds that trail in Acheron
From shores of night and horror; and thy hands,
Like roots of cypresses uptorn in storm
That still retain their grisly provender,
Make the glad wine and manna of the skies
Turn to a qualmish sickness in my veins.

THE GHOUL

And who art thou?—some white-faced fool of God,
With wings that emulate the giddy bird,
And bloodless mouth for ever filled with psalms
In lieu of honest victuals! . . . Askest thou
My name? I am the ghoul Necromalor:
In new-made graves I delve for sustenance,
As man within his turnip-fields; I take
For table the uprooted slab, that bears
The words, "In Pace;" black and curdled blood
Of cadávers is all my cupless wine—
Slow-drunken, as the dainty vampire drinks
From pulses oped in never-ending sleep.

THE SERAPH

O, foulness born as of the ninefold curse
Of dragon-mouthed Apollyon, plumed with darts
And armed with horns of incandescent bronze!
O, dark as Satan's nightmare, or the fruit
Of Belial's rape on hell's black hippogriff!
What knowest *thou* of Paradise, where grow
The gardens of the manna-laden myrrh,
And lotos never known to Ulysses,
Whose fruit provides our long and sateless banquet?
Where boundless fields, unfurrowed and unsown,
Supply for God's own appanage their foison
Of amber-hearted grain, and sesame
Sweeter than nard the Persian air compounds

With frankincense from isles of India!
Where flame-leaved forests infinitely teem
With palms of tremulous opal, from whose tops
Ambrosial honies fall forevermore
In rains of nacred light! Where rise and rise,
Terrace on hyacinthine terrace, hills
Hung with the grapes that drip cerulean wine,
One draught whereof dissolves eternity
In bliss oblivious and supernal dream!

THE GHOUL

To all the meat their bellies most commend,
To all the according wine. For me, I wot,
The cates whereof thou braggest were as wind
In halls where men had feasted yesterday,
Or furbished bones the full hyena leaves.
Tiger and pig have their apportioned glut,
Nor lacks the shark his provender; the bird
Is nourished with the worm of charnels; man,
Or the grey wolf, will slay and eat the bird,
Till wolf and man be carrion for the worm.
What wouldst thou? As the elfin lily does,
Or as the Paphian myrtle, pale with love,
I draw me from the unreluctant dead
The rightful meat my belly's law demands.
Eaters of death are all: Life shall not live,
Save that its food be death: no atomy
In any star, nor heaven's remotest moon
But hath a billion billion times been made
The food of insatiable life, and food
Of death insatiate: for all is change—
Change, that hath wrought the chancre and the rose,
And wrought the star, and wrought the sapphire-stone,
And lit great altars, and the eyes of lions—
Change, that hath made the very gods from slime
Drawn from the pits of Python, and will fling
Gods and their builded heavens back again
To slime. The fruits of archangelic light
Thou braggest of, and grapes of azure wine,
Have been the dung of dragons and the blood

Of toads in Phlegethon: each particle
That is their splendor, clomb in separate ways
Through suns and worlds and cycles infinite—
Through burning brume of systems unbegun,
And manes of long-haired comets, that have lashed
The night of space to fury and to fire;
And in the core of cold and lightless stars,
And in immalleable metals deep,
Each atomy hath slept, or known the slime
Of cyclopean oceans turned to air
Before the suns of Ophiuchus rose;
And they have known the interstellar night,
And they have lain at root of sightless flowers
In worlds without a sun, or at the heart
Of monstrous-eyed and panting flowers of flesh,
Or eon-blooming amaranths of stone;
And they have ministered within the brains
Of sages and magicians, and have served
To swell the pulse of kings and conquerors,
And have been privy to the hearts of queens.

(The Ghoul turns his back on the Seraph, and moves away, singing.)

The Song

O condor, keep thy mountain-ways
Above the long Andean lands;
Gier-eagle, guard the eastern sands
Where the forsaken camel strays:
Beetle and worm and I will ward
The lardered graves of lout and lord.

Oh, warm and bright the blood that lies
Upon the wounded lion's trail!
Hyena, laugh, and jackal, wail,
And ring him round, who turns and dies!
Beetle and worm and I will ward
The lardered graves of lout and lord.

Arms of a wanton girl are good,
Or hands of harp-player and knight:
Breasts of the nun be sweet and white,

Sweet is the festive friar's blood.
Beetle and worm and I will ward
The lardered graves of lout and lord.

The Medusa of Despair

I may not mask for ever with the grace
Of woven flowers thine eyes of staring stone:
Ere the lithe adders and the garlands blown,
Parting their tangle, have disclosed thy face
Lethal as are the pale young suns in space—
Ere my life take the likeness of thine own—
Get hence! the dark gods languish on their throne,
And flameless grow the Furies they embrace.

Regressive, through what realms of elder doom
Where even the swart vans of Time are stunned,
Seek thou some tall Cimmerian citadel,
And proud demonian capitals unsunned
Whose ramparts, ominous with torrent gloom,
Heave worldward on the unwaning light of hell.

A Vision of Lucifer

I saw a shape with human form and face,
If such should in apotheosis stand:
Deep in the shadows of a desolate land
His burning feet obtained colossal base,
And spheral on the lonely arc of space,
His head, a menace unto heavens unspanned,
Arose with towered eyes that might command
The sunless, blank horizon of that place.

And straight I knew him for the mystic one
That is the brother, born of human dream,
Of man rebellious at an unknown rod;
The mind's ideal, and the spirit's sun;
A column of clear flame, in lands extreme,
Set opposite the darkness that is God.

The Witch in the Graveyard

Scene: A forsaken graveyard, by moonlight. Enter two witches.

FIRST WITCH

Sit, sister, now that haggish Hecate
Appropriate and ghastly favor sheds,
And with wild light forwards our enterprise;
And watch the weighted eyelids of each grave,
As never mother watched her babe, to mark,
At zenith of the necromantic moon,
The stir of that disquiet, when the dead,
From suckling nightmares of the charnel dark
Or long insomnia on a mouldy couch,
Impelled like wan somnambulists, arise—
Constrained to emerge and walk, or seated each
On his own tombstone, shrouded council hold,
Or commerce with the sooty wings of hell.
All omens of this influential hour
When all dark powers, thronging to the dark,
Promote enchantment with their wavèd wings,
And brim the wind with potency malign—
A dew of dread to aid our cauldron—these
Observe thou closely, while I seek afield
All requisite swart herbs of venefice
And evil roots unto our usance ripe.

(The first witch departs, leaving the other among the tombs, and returns after a time, in the course of her search.)

FIRST WITCH

Sister, what seest or what hearest thou?

SECOND WITCH

                        I see
The moonlight, and the slowly moving gleam
That westers hour by hour on tomb and stone;
And shrivelled lilies, tossed i' the winter's breath
With their attenuate shadows, as might dance
Phantom with flaffing phantom; at my side,

The white and shuddering grasses of the grave,
With nettles, and the parching fumitory,
Whose leaves, root-trellised on the bones of death,
Will rasp and bristle to the lightest wind.

    (The first witch moves on, and approaches again, after an interval.)

First Witch

Sister, what seest or what hearest thou?

Second Witch

                I see
The mound-stretched gossamers, cradles to the dew;
Moon-wefted briers, and the cypress-trees
With shadow swathed, or cerements of the moon;
And corpse-lights borne from aisle to secret aisle
Within the footless forest. . . .

              Now I hear
The lich-owl, shrieking lethal prophecy;
And whimpering winds, the children of the air,
Lost in the glades of mystery and gloom.

    (The first witch disappears, and passes again shortly.)

First Witch

Sister, what seest or what hearest thou?

Second Witch

                I see
The ghost-white owl, with huge, sulphureous eyes,
That veers in prone, unwhispered flight, and hear
The small shriek of the moon-adventuring mole,
Gripped in mid-graveyard. . . . And I see
Where some wild shadow shakes, though the pale wind
Of midnight stirs far off . . . and hear
Curst mandragores that gibber to the moon,
Though no man treads anigh. . . .
    (After an interval)
Some predal hand doth hold the wandering air;
Now dies the throttled wind with rattling breath,

And round about a breathing Silence prowls.
   (After another interval)
I hear the cheeping of the bat-lipped ghouls,
Aroused beneath the vaulted cypresses
Far off; and lipless muttering of tombs,
With clash of bones bestirred in ancient charnels
Beneath their shroud of unclean light that crawls. . . .
Earth shudders, and rank odours 'gin to rise
From tombs a-crack; and shaken out all at once
From mid-air, and directly 'neath the moon,
Meseems what hanging wing divides the light,
Like a black film of mist, or thickest shadow:
But on the tomb there is no shadow!

First Witch

Enough! 'twill be a prosperous night, methinks,
For commerce of the demons with the dead,
And for us too, when every omen's good,
And fraught with promise of a potent brew.

The Flight of Azrael

Scene: An immense and darkling plain, remotely lit by the sunset of the last day. Two demons, passing from the interstellar deep, have paused on an isolated hill-top.

First Demon

What world is this, all desolate and dim
Under the lone, phantasmagoric heavens
Great with the hanging night? Yon luminance
Is lurid as the furnace-glare of hell,
Seen from the contiguity of gloom
Of a Cimmerian region. All the air
Flags heavily, as beneath the weight of wings
Invisible and evil—from the plain
No movement, save of shadows mustering.
Beyond the heels of day.

SECOND DEMON
                    It is the Earth,
A hoary planet, old in wrath and woe
As any hell. Red pestilence and war
Have now refunded to the usuring wind
The breath of all its peoples; Azrael,
Delivering now the town and necropole
To one decay in night's abysmal vault,
Prepares him for departure. From afar,
Seest thou not the towering of his wings,
Like thunder on the sunset? Widening,
Those vans involve and stifle half the light
With bat-like folds and ribs: on the further stars,
Or worlds unknown of the outer infinite,
He now intends the darkness of his course;
On Algol's planets haply poised, he will
Make permanent the sable sun's eclipse,
Or round some vast Antarean satellite
His shadowed arc will broaden to a sphere,
Oblivion's black and perfect globe. . . . On Earth
He comes no more: the very worms have died
In the scarce-nibbled carrion; the thin wind
Will write man's epitaph in shifting sand,
And the pale unfading arabesques of frost
Adorn and fret his ghoul-forgotten tomb.

The Mummy

From out the light of many a mightier day,
From Pharaonic splendour, Memphian gloom,
And from the night aeonian of the tomb
They brought him forth, to meet the modern ray—
Upon his brow the unbroken seal of clay,
While gods have gone to a forgotten doom,
And desolation and the dust assume
Temple and cot immingling in decay.

From out the everlasting womb sublime
Of cyclopean death, within a land
Of tombs and cities rotting in the sun,

He is reborn to mock the might of time,
While kings have built against Oblivion
With walls and columns of the windy sand.

Minatory

Scorners of the Muse, beware!
She that you deny is queen
Of a thunder-girt demesne
In the worlds of Otherwhere:
Ships that ply on shadowy seas
Past the surging galaxies,
Bring the loot of heaven and hell
To her stellar citadel;
Powers benignant and malign
In her single service join,
Cherubim and seraphim
Wait upon her briefest whim;
Gods august you have not known
Gather to her awful throne,
Demons that you wot not of
Serve her with a fearful love;
Dim Summanus, lord of night,
Is her moiling minister,
Demogorgon toils for her
In the darkling Infinite.

To the Chimera

Unknown chimera, take us, for we tire
Amid the known monotony of things!
Descend, and bearing sunward with bright wings
Our mournful weariness and sad desire,

Pause not to prove the opal shores untrod,
Below thee fading, and the fields of rose;
Till on thy horns of planished silver flows
The sanguine light of Edens lost to God.

There, for the weary sense insatiate,
Primeval sleep from towering scarlet blooms

Would fall in slow and infinite perfumes;

Or we could leave thy crystal wings elate—
Riding the pagan plain with knees that press
The golden flanks of some great centauress.

The Whisper of the Worm

How long, O soul, hast parleyed with the worm—
Hearing how long the whisper subtle-sweet
From out the dust thy Sisyphean feet
Must darkly vex and travel for a term?

"Lie down with me: supreme and sole release
I proffer, from the weariness of things,
From ways where with no serpent-staff nor wings
Thou pantest still; I am the way of peace.

"Lie down with me, lie down, and thou shalt know
The secret known to slave and Pharaoh,
And win the final wisdom of the dead:

"Like couches amaranthine-piled and deep
Where love may lie, by pleasure laid asleep,
I make the mould or marble of thy bed."

The Envoys

None other saw them when they came
Across the many-clangored mart,
But in mine eyes and in my heart
They passed as might the pillared flame
Of lightning loosened on the tombs,
Or errant suns that wander by
To dawn on the Cimmerii.

Great monarchs, proud and cypress-tall,
With zones and crowns of argentry,
They were, who proffered royally
Full urns of pulsing gems to all:—
The blood-warm gems of lunar wombs,
Pale ores, and opals pavonine,
And beryls like to leopards' eyne.

Their eyes were lit with alien day,
Were filled of alien worlds; their feet
With starry splendors paved the street,
And silver dust of some bright way
Fell from their garments, with perfumes
More strange than breath of vernal gales
From Saturn's moly-cinctured vales.

What embassy were they, from suns
Of Algebar or Capricorn—
From planets of remoter morn
In flaming fields where Taurus runs—
Or haply come, immediate,
From out a four-dimensioned world
With the occlusive ether furled?

They strode upon the swooning pave,
They towered by the trembling spires,
Tall as apocalyptic fires
Above the peoples of the grave:
But, sightless and inveterate,
To Mammon vowed, the throng went by,
Charneled beneath an iron sky.

Yea, blinder than the steel and stone,
Men took not from their proffered store
One gift of all the gifts they bore,
But sued for gold to gods foreknown.
I, too, bemused, inebriate,
Amort with splendor, could but stand
And see them pass, with empty hand.

Nyctalops

Ye that see in darkness
When the moon is drowned
In the coiling fen-mist
Far along the ground—
Ye that see in darkness,
Say, what have ye found?

—We have seen strange atoms
Trysting on the air—
The dust of vanished lovers
Long parted in despair,
And dust of flowers that withered
In worlds of otherwhere.

We have seen the nightmares
Winging down the sky,
Bat-like and silent,
To where the sleepers lie;
We have seen the bosoms
Of the succubi.

We have seen the crystal
Of dead Medusa's tears.
We have watched the undines
That wane in stagnant weirs,
And mandrakes madly dancing
By black, blood-swollen meres.

We have seen the satyrs
Their ancient loves renew
With moon-white nymphs of cypress,
Pale dryads of the yew,
In the tall grass of graveyards
Weighed down with evening's dew.

We have seen the darkness
Where charnel things decay,
Where atom moves with atom
In shining swift array,
Like ordered constellations
On some sidereal way.

We have seen fair colors
That dwell not in the light—
Intenser gold and iris
Occult and recondite;
We have seen the black suns
Pouring forth the night.

Jungle Twilight

From teak and tamarind and palm
The heavy sun goes down unseen;
The jungle drowns in duskier green;
And quickening perfumes vespertine
Alone assail the sluggish calm.

Narcotic silence, opiate gloom:
The painted parakeets are gone,
The blazoned butterflies withdrawn.
Nocturnal blossoms, weird and wan,
Like phantom wings and faces bloom.

In the high trees the darkness grows,
And, rising, overbrims the sky.
Like a black serpent gliding by
'Neath woven creepers covertly,
Unknown and near, the river flows;

Where deeplier in oblivion's tide
The dateless, fair pagodas fall,
And, winding on the toppled wall
Where carven gods hold carnival,
The cobra couples with his bride.

Necromancy

My heart is made a necromancer's glass,
Where homeless forms and exile phantoms teem,
Where faces of forgotten sorrows gleam
And dead despairs archaic peer and pass:
Grey longings of some weary heart that was
Possess me, and the multiple, supreme,
Unwildered hope and star-emblazoned dream
Of questing armies. . . . Ancient queen and lass,
Risen vampire-like from out the wormy mould,
Deep in the magic mirror of my heart
Behold their perished beauty, and depart.
And now, from black aphelions far and cold,
Swimming in deathly light on charnel skies,
The enormous ghosts of bygone worlds arise.

The Witch with Eyes of Amber

I met a witch with amber eyes
Who slowly sang a scarlet rune,
Shifting to an icy laughter
Like the laughter of the moon.

Red as a wanton's was her mouth,
And fair the breast she bade me take
With a word that clove and clung
Burning like a furnace-flake.

But from her bright and lifted bosom,
When I touched it with my hand,
Came the many-needled coldness
Of a glacier-taken land.

And, lo! the witch with eyes of amber
Vanished like a blown-out flame,
Leaving but the lichen-eaten
Stone that bore a blotted name.

Cambion

I am that spawn of witch and demon
By time's mad prophets long foretold:
The unnamed fear of king and freeman,
I roam the lawless outland wold,
Couching amid the weeds and mould
With dire Alecto for my leman.

I am that hidden piper, playing
The Pan-like strains of malefice
That lure the lonely traveler, straying
Upon the crumbling precipice:
To filmed morass or blind abyss
His feet must follow, never staying.

I am that swart, unseen pursuer
Whose lust begets a changeling breed:
All women know me for their wooer:
Mine is the whisper maidens heed
At twilight; mine the spells that lead

The matron to the nighted moor.
I am that messenger whose call
Convenes dark mage and banished lord
And branded witch and whip-flayed thrall,
To plot, amid the madness poured
On the black Sabbat's frothing horde,
The bale of realms, the planet's fall.

The Saturnienne

Beneath the skies of Saturn, pale and many-mooned,
Her palace is;
Her wyvern-warded spires of celadon, enruned
With names benign and mightier names of malefice,
Illume with saffron phares
A marish by the black, lethargic seas lagooned;
Her dragon-holden stairs
Go down in coiling jet and gold on some unplumbed abyss.

Long as a leaping flame, exalted over all,
Across the sun
Her banners bear Aidennic blooms armorial
And beasts infernal on a field of ciclaton;
Amid her agate courts,
Like to a demon ichor, towering proud and tall,
A scarlet fountain spurts,
To fall upon parterres of dwale and deathly hebenon.

From out her amber windows, gazing languidly
On a weird land
Where conium and cannabis and upas-tree
Seem wrought in verdigris against the copper sand,
She sees and sees again
A trailing salt like leprous dragons from the sea
Far-crawled upon the fen;
And foam of monster-cloven gulfs beyond a fallow strand.

Or, looking from her turrets to the south and north,
She notes the gleam
Of molied mountains and of rivers pouring forth,
Clear as the dawn, to fail in fulvous rill and stream

The widening waste amid;
Or swell the fallen meres, abominable, swarth,
In green mirages hid,
To be the unquested grails of hell, of death and deathful dream.

Chance

Bow down before the daemon of the world—
This monstrous god, half-idiot and half-ape,
With fumbling hands omnipotent to shape
A harlot's breast or build great altars. Hurled
From the lost sun to sunless hell, or whirled
Back to their heaven with equal jest and jape,
All other gods shall nevermore escape
His will that once begot them. Wars unfurled
With banners blown like ever-wandering fires
From realm to realm conflagrant, or the play
Of coupling mice or monsters, wake alway
To his dominion. Darkly born thereof,
The troubling atoms teem to stars and byres,
The leper's flesh, the white flesh of thy love.

Revenant

I am the spectre who returns
Unto some desolate world in ruin borne afar
On the black flowing of Lethean skies:
Ever I search, in cryptic galleries,
The void sarcophagi, the broken urns
Of many a vanished avatar;
Or haunt the gloom of crumbling pylons vast
In temples that enshrine the shadowy past.
Viewless, impalpable, and fleet,
I roam stupendous avenues, and greet
Familiar sphinxes carved from everlasting stone,
Or the fair, brittle gods of long ago,
Decayed and fallen low.
And there I mark the tall clepsammiae
That time has overthrown,

And empty clepsydrae,
And dials drowned in umbrage never-lifting;
And there, on rusty parapegms,
I read the ephemerides
Of antique stars and elder planets drifting
Oblivionward in night;
And there, with purples of the tomb bedight
And crowned with funereal gems,
I hold awhile the throne
Whereon mine immemorial selves have sate,
Canopied by the triple-tinted glory
Of the three suns forever paled and flown.

I am the spectre who returns
And dwells content with his forlorn estate
In mansions lost and hoary
Where no lamp burns;
Who trysts within the sepulchre,
And finds the ancient shadows lovelier
Than gardens all emblazed with sevenfold noon,
Or topaz-builded towers
That throng below some iris-pouring moon.
Exiled and homeless in the younger stars,
Henceforth I shall inhabit that grey clime
Whose days belong to primal calendars;
Nor would I come again
Back to the garish terrene hours:
For I am free of vaults unfathomable
And treasures lost from time:
With bat and vampire there
I flit through sombre skies immeasurable
Or fly adown the unending subterranes;
Mummied and ceremented,
I sit in councils of the kingly dead,
And oftentimes for vestiture I wear
The granite of great idols looming darkly
In atlantean fanes;
Or closely now and starkly
I cling as clings the attenuating air
About the ruins bare.

Song of the Necromancer

I will repeat a subtle rune—
And thronging suns of Otherwhere
Shall blaze upon the blinded air,
And spectres terrible and fair
Shall walk the riven world at noon.

The star that was mine empery
Is dust upon unwinnowed skies:
But primal dreams have made me wise,
And soon the shattered years shall rise
To my remembered sorcery.

To mantic mutterings, brief and low,
My palaces shall lift amain,
My bowers bloom; I will regain
The lips whereon my lips have lain
In rose-red twilights long ago.

Before my murmured exorcism
The world, a wispy wraith, shall flee:
A stranger earth, a weirder sea,
Peopled with shapes of Faëry,
Shall swell upon the waste abysm.

The pantheons of darkened stars
Shall file athwart the crocus dawn;
Goddess and Gorgon, Lar and faun,
Shall tread the amaranthine lawn,
And giants fight their thunderous wars.

Like graven mountains of basalt,
Dark idols of my demons there
Shall tower through bright zones of air,
Fronting the sun with level stare;
And hell shall pave my deepest vault.

Phantom and fiend and sorcerer
Shall serve me . . . till my term shall pass,
And I become no more, alas,
Than a frail shadow on the glass
Before some latter conjurer.

Pour chercher du nouveau

Call up the lordly daemon that in Cimmeria dwells
Amid the vaults untrodden, long-sealed with lethal spells,
Amid the untouched waters of Lemur-warded wells.

Call up the wiser genius who knows and understands
The lore of night and limbo, who finds in tomb-dark lands
The pearls and shells and wreckage that strew the dawnless strands—

Remnants of elder cargoes, lost, enigmatic spars
From seas without horizon, washing occulted stars,
From shadow-sunken cycles of vaster calendars.

Call up the vagrant daemon, whose vans have haply strayed
Through subterranean heavens by dead Anubis bayed,
Who has seen abysmal evil, aloof and undismayed;

Beholding fouler phantoms no necromancer wakes,
Reptilian bulks that cumber the thick putrescent lakes,
And pterodactyls brooding their nests in charnel brakes;

Hearing the unspent anger of troglodyte and Goth,
The rote of gods abolished, the moan of Ashtaroth,
The hunger and the fury of famished Behemoth.

Call up the sapient daemon, whose eyes have haply read
The cipher-graven portals in planets of the dead,
Who knows the dark apastrons of stars for ever sped;

Who has seen the lost eidola hewn from no earthly stone,
The unrusting magic mirrors, in chambers chill and lone,
That hold supernal faces from heavens overthrown;

Who has heard the vatic voices of witch-wrought teraphim,
The wailing fires of Moloch, the flames that swirl and swim
Around the blood-black altars of ravening Baalim;

Who has heard the sands of ocean, far-sifted on the beach,
Repeating crystal echoes of some sidereal speech;
Who has heard the atoms telling their legend each to each.

Call up the errant daemon, the pilgrim of strange lands,
And he will come, arising from shadow-tided strands,
With gifts of bale and beauty and wonder in his hands.

Witch-Dance

Between the windy, swirling fire
And all the stillness of the moon,
Sweet witch, you danced at my desire,
Turning some weird and lovely rune
To paces like the swirling fire.

As in the Sabbat's ancient round
With strange and subtle steps you went;
And toward the heavens and toward the ground
Your steeple-shapen hat was bent
As in the Sabbat's ancient round.

Upon the earth your paces wrought
A circle such as magians made . . .
And still some hidden thing you sought
With hands desirous, half afraid,
Beyond the ring your paces wrought.

Your supple youth and loveliness
A glamor left upon the air:
Whether to curse, whether to bless,
You wrought a stronger magic there
With your lithe youth and loveliness.

Your fingers, on the smoke and flame,
Moved in mysterious conjuring;
You seemed to call a silent Name,
And lifted like an outstretched wing
Your somber gown against the flame.

What darkling and demonian Lord,
In fear or triumph, did you call?
Ah! was it then that you implored,
With secret signs equivocal,
The coming of the covens' Lord?

Sweet witch, you conjured forth my heart
To answer always at your will!
Like Merlin, in some place apart,
It lies enthralled and captive still:
Sweet witch, you conjured thus my heart!

Not Theirs the Cypress-Arch

Dream not the dead will wait,
Slow-crumbling in the allotted ground,
Nor rise except to some sonorous trump
And searing splendors of the doomsday sun:
They rise, they gather about us now,
Crowding the quiet day.

To us, entombed in time,
Asleep within a vaster vault,
They use a speech we seem not to have known,
Yet guide us like sleep-walkers to and fro—
By those forgotten voices drawn
With secret tacit guile.

Not theirs the cypress-arch,
The sexton's haunt, the hallowed stones,
The charnel morris stilled by chanticleer:
Dark demons, through the forum and the street
They move, and we, their fleshly ghosts,
Like driven demoniacs are.

III. The Eldritch Dark

A Song from Hell

This song I got me from the nether pits,
Where, as a witches' cauldron-brew, that blends
Envenomed roots and herbs malignly foul,
With poison-essence drawn from charnel things,
And carrion found by night, the various damned
Bubble and seethe with their own agony,
And cry to upward firmamental gulfs
(Reddened with blotching flame as though with stars)
A chant that rears like some distillment weird,
Atwist with urge of pain from writhing lips:—

We are the damned—the stain and moil
That Death has washed from earthly time;
Drawn down by tides of Hell, we boil
Like toads within a torrid slime.

Our sins were great—a deadly charge—
And yet less heavy than our fate:
We pour through Hell's alembic large,
Each soul transformed to vital hate;

The good that in our hearts remained
By sin untainted, now is one
With vileness cankeringly ingrained;
By earth and Hell we stand undone—

For that which earth unfinished left,
The consummation of the pit.
From out the insuperable cleft,
To where its lords presiding sit,

And watch with calm contestless sight,
We burn, by double test refined

To clearest evil—purgèd quite
Of food or mercy from the mind.

Our souls are linked to vast despair,
As to some nadir-founded rock,
Where never hope descends to mock
Beyond the dip of terrene air.

We heighten to a hate that beats
In rage all impotently strong
Against the worlds that league with wrong,
Whose pain each other's pain completes.

Ah, would our hate were hands to draw
The lords of earth and hell beneath!
Ah, would our hate were venomed teeth
To rend them through their mail of law!

Ah, would that we might cleave with hate
The roof, and base, and walls of Hell—
Wrench at its pillars till they fell
With ruin indiscriminate!

Immovably it stands, with springs
Of fire to tear its inward glooms,
Wherefrom, ascending high, our fumes
Are breath of incense to its kings.

The Titans in Tartarus

Low in the far-flung shadow of the world,
Under the moveless stretch of glooms great-wing'd
That brood the abyss, vague Tartarus lapsed remote
Through zones of spacial silence. Night and Time,
Agreeing once, had made thereof a place
Immediate unto Chaos, and removed
From temporal clamor and terrestrial hush,
In gulfs world-sundered from the sun. Far up
Light was, a gossamer of frailest blue,
Above the lift of Cyclopean walls,
And flight of crags incredible through heavens
Of darkness, and ethereal space of eve,

Sheer, everlasting. But within the abyss
The silence of the death of suns was come,
And the far light seemed as the ghost of days
Flown and forgotten; or as memory
Sent through the drifts of drear Oblivion
To the forgetful dead. But unto them,
The fall'n Titanic gods disconsolate,
It shone as might a throne supreme and lost—
Phantasmal, unattainable, athwart
The chasm of downfall and defeat. Apart
In the waste darkness round, the purblind air
Scarcely their presence each to each betrayed,
Who, to the gaze of those but newly fallen,
Had seemed as clouds upon a moonless midnight—
Black, formless, without substance, motionless.
The flaming tumult of disastrous fight,
Taking their outward fire, had left them bleak
As their own statues, who yet ached within.
And battle-splendours gloomed with rust were strewn
Around them, where the darkness heeded not
If rust or clearest splendours were: downcast
Were ineffectual blade and useless mail,
Left to the barren and devouring dust
That knew not nor should know the sun.

          Abrupt
The change, from impact and surprise of strife—
From the embattled world, where searing war
Had lately flamed through indecisive lands
Open to sun and stars—to this drear deep,
This unity of night and misery,
Of desolation, silence, and defeat
Intolerable, sure. Speechless beneath
That gloom the Titans lay, where like the strong
Suspense of noiseless and enormous wings,
Immediate breathless menace infinite,
Came hideous, myriad-eyed Despair. With minds
Tortured, and anguished gaze, they saw the dark
Writhe to unnumbered forms of subtlest fear,
Such terrors as attend the night of suns
For the strange impotence of gods dethroned,

The face of Chaos with a thousand leers,
And phantoms pointing at eternal gulfs.

Dark with defeat, gigantically dumb,
Like Memnons morningless, that have survived
The dawn-voiced vibrant sun's last silencing,
The Titans waited. Time, that hath for hue
In the swift light and cloud-surprise of Change,
All iris that enchants the sunset foam,
Now, with grey silence clad, dismal and slow,
Through the grey darkness waned, as one that hath
No hope, foreworn upon an endless way.
All desolation and all hopelessness
Had hushed, it seemed, a deep that was the tomb—
So huge that dark—of all magnificence,
Aeons of splendour, whole antiquities
Of Time-forgotten glories. There the gods,
Sleepless in midst as of Oblivion,
Abiding, fronted anguish infinite,
And all the strong renewal of despair
Throughout Tartarean, dark eternity.

The Twilight Woods

As eve to purple turns the afterglow
That lately with a rich and fervent red
Illumed the sunset skies, my feet are led
By whispering spirits of the winds that blow
At this grey hour, and many secrets know,
To where the oaks and pines meet overhead
In plots to keep away the light. I tread
Beneath their archways pensively and slow.

Here darkening twilight is a sorcery
Whereby all things are rendered weird and strange:
Bushes and trees fantastic shapes assume,
And shadows lurk within the forest's range
Felt but unseen, for when I turn they flee
To darker depths of consecrated gloom.

Lethe

I flow beneath the columns that upbear
The world, and all of heaven and limbo and hell;
Foamless I glide, where sounds nor glimmers tell
My motion nadirward: no moment's flare
Gives each to each the shapes that, unaware,
Convening upon my verge, essay the spell
Of essential night-thick waters that compel
One face from pain and rapture and despair.

The fruitless earth's denied and cheated sons
Meet here, where fruitful and unfruitful cease.
And when their lords, the mightier, hidden Ones,
Have drained all worlds, till being's wine is low,
Shall they not come, and from the oblivious flow
Drink at one draft a universe of peace?

Atlantis

Above its domes the gulfs accumulate.
Far up, the sea-gales blare their bitter screed:
But here the buried waters take no heed—
Deaf, and with welded lips pressed down by weight
Of the upper ocean. Dim, interminate,
In cities over-webbed with somber weed,
Where galleons crumble and the krakens breed,
The slow tide coils through sunken court and gate.

From out the ocean's phosphor-starry dome,
A ghostly light is dubitably shed
On altars of a goddess garlanded
With blossoms of some weird and hueless vine;
And, wingèd, fleet, through skies beneath the foam,
Like silent birds the sea-things dart and shine.

The Eldritch Dark

Now as the twilight's doubtful interval
Closes with night's accomplished certainty,
A wizard wind goes crying eerily,

And on the wold misshapen shadows crawl,
Miming the trees, whose voices climb and fall,
Imploring, in Sabbatic ecstasy,
The sky where vapor-mounted phantoms flee
From the scythed moon impendent over all.

Twin veils of covering cloud and silence, thrown
Across the movement and the sound of things,
Make blank the night, till in the broken west
The moon's ensanguined blade awhile is shown. . . .
The night grows whole again. . . . The shadows rest,
Gathered beneath a greater shadow's wings.

White Death

Methought the world was bound with final frost:
The sun, made hueless as with fear and awe,
Illumined still the lands it could not thaw.
Then on my road, with instant evening crost,
Death stood, and in its dusky veils enwound,
Mine eyes forgot the light, until I came
Where poured the inseparate, unshadowed flame
Of phantom suns in self-irradiance drowned.

Death lay revealed in all its haggardness:
Immitigable wastes horizonless;
Profundities that held nor bar nor veil;
All hues wherewith the suns and world were dyed
In light invariable nullified;
All darkness rendered shelterless and pale.

A Dead City

Twilight ascends the abandoned ramps of noon
Within an ancient land, whose after-time
Unfathomably shadows its ruined prime.
Like rising mist the night increases soon
Round shattered palaces, ere yet the moon
On mute, unsentried walls and turrets climb,
And touch with pallor of sepulchral rime
The desert where a city's bones are strewn.

She comes at last: unsepultured, they show
In all the hoary starkness of old stone.
From out a shadow like the lips of Death
Issues a wind, that through the ruins blown,
Cries like a prophet's ghost, with wailing breath,
The weirds of finished and forgotten woe.

The Cloud-Islands

What islands marvellous are these,
That gem the sunset's tides of light—
Opals aglow in saffron seas?
How beautiful they lie, and bright,
Like some new-found Hesperides!

What varied, changing magic hues
Tint gorgeously each shore and hill!
What blazing, vivid golds and blues
Their seaward winding valleys fill!
What amethysts their peaks suffuse!

Close held by curving arms of land
That out within the ocean reach,
I mark a faery city stand,
Set high upon a sloping beach
That burns with fire of shimmering sand.

Of sunset-light is formed each wall;
Each dome a rainbow-bubble seems;
And every spire that towers tall
A ray of golden moonlight gleams;
Of opal-flame in every hall.

Alas! how quickly dims their glow!
What veils their dreamy splendours mar!
Like broken dreams the islands go,
As down from strands of cloud and star,
The sinking tides of daylight flow.

The City of the Titans

I saw a city in a lonely land;
Foursquare, it fronted upon gulfs of fire;
Behind, the night of Erebus hung entire;
And deserts gloomed or glimmered on each hand.

Sunken it seemed, past any star or sun,
Yet strong with bastion, proud with tower and dome:
An archetypal, Titan-builded Rome,
Dread, thunder-named, the seat of gods foredone.

Outreaching time, beyond destruction based,
Immensely piled upon the prostrate waste
And cinctured with insuperable deeps,

The city dreamed in darkness evermore,
Pregnant with crypts of terrible strange lore
And doom-fraught arsenals in lampless keeps.

The City of Destruction

(A Fragment)

I

The incognizable kings of Night, within their unrevealed abyss,
Have built them a metropolis against the kingdoms of the light.

Its mountain-passing ramparts climb exalted from the nadir flats
In black, Babelian ziggurats that tier the dusk of nether time.

Prodigious, dire and indistinct, with horns that lift the heavens' doom,
Its turrets crowd the skyless gloom huge as the night of hells extinct.

The hostile gulfs for armor wear its walls as of a thousand Romes;
The swollen menace of its domes enhelms the swart, inimic air.

The Powers to darkness ministrant have fortressed them supremely well,
Building their dreadful citadel with massed, eternal adamant

Quarried from the core entire of suns that night and ice entomb;
Their secret furnaces relume the stone that once was stellar fire.

The monstrous lamps of Death and Mars like demon moons emblaze their
    halls;
The watch-fires on the infernal walls flame like a crown of fallen stars.

II

From out the sunken courts resound colossal engineries of doom;
Some slow, malign, tremendous loom dismally rumbles underground;

Loud shuttles clack implacably; unknown machines, with clangorous ire,
Beat in their hearts of throbbing fire the instants of eternity;

The crooked arms of titan cranes, with grasp Briarean, momently
Lift to the dim, Tartarean sky a nameless freight in stretchèd chains;

And Acheronian waters roar, constrained, relentless, subterrene,
Where at their evil toil unseen the hellish wheels moan evermore.

Beyond the Great Wall

Beyond the far Cathayan wall,
A thousand leagues athwart the sky,
The scarlet stars and mornings die,
The gilded moons and sunsets fall.

Across the sulphur-colored sands
With bales of silk the camels fare,
Harnessed with vermeil and with vair,
Into the blue and burning lands.

And ah, the song the drivers sing
To while the desert leagues away—
A song they sang in old Cathay
Ere youth had left the eldest king,

Ere love and beauty both grew old
And wonder and romance were flown
On irised wings to worlds unknown,
To stars of undiscovered gold.

And I their alien words would know,
And follow past the lonely wall
Where gilded moons and sunsets fall,
As in a song of long ago.

Solution

The ghostly fire that walks the fen,
Tonight thine only light shall be;
On lethal ways thy soul shall pass,
And prove the stealthy, coiled morass
With mocking mists for company.

On roads thou goest not again,
To shores where thou hast never gone,
Fare onward, though the shuddering queach
And serpent-rippled waters reach
Like seepage-pools of Acheron

Beside thee; and the twisten reeds,
Close-raddled as a witch's net,
Enwind thy knees, and cling and clutch
Like wreathing adders; though the touch
Of the blind air be dank and wet

As from a wounded Thing that bleeds
In cloud and darkness overhead—
Fare onward, where thy dreams of yore
In splendor drape the fetid shore
And pestilential waters dead.

And though the toads' irrision rise
Like grinding of Satanic racks,
And spectral willows, gaunt and grey,
Gibber along thy shrouded way,
Where vipers lie with livid backs

And watch thee with their sulphurous eyes—
Fare onward, till thy feet shall slip
Deep in the sudden pool ordained,
And all the noisome draught be drained
That turns to Lethe on the lip.

Rosa Mystica

The secret rose we vainly dream to find
Was blown in grey Atlantis long ago,
Or in old summers of the realms of snow

Its attar lulled the pole-arisen wind;
Or once its broad and breathless petals pined
In gardens of Persepolis, aglow
With fiery-sworded sunlight and the slow
Red waves of sand, invincible and blind.

On orient isles or isles hesperian,
Through mystic days ere mortal time began,
It flowered above the ever-flowering foam;
Or, legendless, in lands of yesteryear,
It flamed among the violets—near, how near
To unenchanted fields and hills of home!

Symbols

No more of gold and marble, nor of snow
And sunlight and vermilion, would I make
My vision and my symbols, nor would take
The auroral flame of some prismatic floe.
Nor iris of the frail and lunar bow,
Flung on the shafted waterfalls that wake
The night's blue slumber in a shadowy lake.
To body forth my fantasies, and show
Communicable mystery, I would find,
In adamantine darkness of the earth,
Metals untouched of any sun; and bring
Black azures of the nether sea to birth—
Or fetch the secret, splendid leaves, and blind
Blue lilies of an Atlantean spring.

The City in the Desert

In a lost land, that only dreams have known,
Where flaming suns walk naked and alone;
Among horizons bright as molten brass,
And glowing heavens like furnaces of glass,
It rears with dome and tower manifold,
Rich as a dawn of amarant and gold,
Or gorgeous as the Phoenix, born of fire,
And soaring from an opalescent pyre

Sheer to the zenith. Like some anademe
Of Titan jewels turned to flame and dream
The city crowns the far horizon-light
Over the flowered meads of damassin. . . .
A desert isle of madreperl! wherein
The thurifer and opal-fruited palm
And heaven-thronging minarets becalm
The seas of azure wind. . . .

(*Note*: These lines were remembered out of a dream, and are given verbatim.)

The Melancholy Pool

Marked by that priesthood of the Night's misrule,
The shadow-cowled, imprecatory trees—
Cypress that guarded woodland secrecies
And graves that waited the delaying ghoul,
Nathless I neared the melancholy pool,
Chief care of all, but closelier sentinelled
By those whose roots were deepest in dead eld.
Where the thwart-woven boughs were wet and cool
As with a mist of poison, I drew near
To mark the tired stars peer dimly down
Through riven branches from the height of space,
And shudder in those waters with quick fear,
Where in black deeps the pale moon seemed to drown—
A haggard girl, with dead, despairing face.

Twilight on the Snow

Before the hill's high altar bowed,
The trees are Druids, weird and white,
Facing the vision of the light
With ancient lips to silence vowed.

No certain sound the woods aver,
Nor motion save of formless wings—
Filled with phantasmal flutterings,
With thronging gloom and shadow-stir.

Unseen, unheard, amid the dell
Lie all the winds that mantic trees
Have lulled with crystal warlockries
And bound about with Merlin-spell.

The Land of Evil Stars

'Neath blue days, and gold, and green,
Blooms the glorious land serene,
Flaming shields of dawns between;
And the rapt white flowers suffice
To illume
With their bright eyes
Fluctuant ecstatic gloom
'Twixt the fallen emerald sun
And the unrisen azure one.

But the season of the night
Comes in all the suns' despite;
And, ah, gorgeous then their sorrows
At departure into morrows
Of remoter lands forgot—
Until now remembered not
For the lovelier flowers of this,
And each lake's pure lucency,
And recalled regretfully,
Regretfully, for leaving *this*.

In the star-possessèd night
The land knows another light—
All the small and evil rays
Of the sorcerous orbs ablaze
With ecstatical intense
Hate and still malevolence—
Dwelling on the fields below
From the ascendancy of even
Till the suns, re-entering heaven,
Glorify with triple glow
The dim flowers smitten low.

Ah, not cold, or kind, as ours,
The stars of those remotest hours!
Peace and pallor of the flowers
They have fevered, they have marred
With the poison of their light,
With distillèd bale and blight
Of a red, accurst regard:
All the toil of sunlight hours
They undo
With their wild eyes—
Eldritch and ecstatic eyes,
Stooping timeward from the skies,
Burning redly in the dew.

Memnon at Midnight

Methought upon the tomb-encumbered shore
I stood of Egypt's lone monarchal stream,
And saw immortal Memnon, throned supreme
In gloom as of that Memphian night of yore:
Fold upon fold purpureal he wore,
Beneath the star-borne canopy extreme—
Carven of silence and colossal dream,
Where waters flowed like sleep forevermore.

Lo, in the darkness, thick with dust of years,
How many a ghostly god around his throne,
With thronging wings that were forgotten Fames,
Stood, ere the dawn restore to ancient ears
The long-withholden thunder of their names,
And music stilled to monumental stone.

The Kingdom of Shadows

A crownless king who reigns alone,
I live within this ashen land,
Where winds rebuild from wandering sand
My columns and my crumbled throne.

My sway is on the men that were,
And wan sweet women, dear and dead;

Beside a marble queen, my bed
Is made within the sepulcher.

In gardens desolate to the sun,
Faring alone, I sigh to find
The dusty closes, dim and blind,
Where winter and the spring are one.

My shadowy visage, grey with grief,
In sunken waters walled with sand,
I see—where all mine ancient land
Lies yellow like an autumn leaf.

My silver lutes of subtle string
Are rust—but on the grievous breeze
I hear what sobbing memories,
And muted sorrows murmuring!

Across the broken monuments,
Memorial of the dreams of old,
The sunset flings a ghostly gold
To mock mine ancient affluence.

About the tombs of stone and brass
The silver lights of evening flee;
And slowly now, and solemnly,
I see the pomp of shadows pass.

Often, beneath some fervid moon,
With splendid spells I vainly strive
Dead loves imperial to revive,
And speak a heart-remembered rune—

But, ah, the lovely phantoms fail,
The faces fade to mist and light,
The vermeil lips of my delight
Are dim, the eyes are ashen-pale.

A crownless king who reigns alone,
I live within this ashen land,
Where winds rebuild from wandering sand
My columns and my crumbled throne.

Moon-Dawn

The hills, a-throng with swarthy pine,
Press up the pale and hollow sky,
And the squat cypresses on high
Reach from the lit horizon-line.

They reach, they reach, with gnarlèd hands—
Malignant hags, obscene and dark—
While the red moon, a demons' ark,
Is borne along the mystic lands.

Outlanders

By desert-deepened wells and chasmed ways,
And noon-high passes of the crumbling nome
Where the fell sphinx and martichoras roam;
Over black mountains lit by meteor-blaze,
Through darkness ending not in solar days,
Beauty, the centauress, has brought us home
To shores where chaos climbs in starry foam,
And the white horses of Polaris graze.

We gather, upon those gulfward beaches rolled,
Driftage of worlds not shown by any chart;
And pluck the fabled moly from wild scaurs:
Though these are scorned by human wharf and mart—
And scorned alike the red, primeval gold
For which we fight the griffins in strange wars.

Warning

Hast heard the voices of the fen,
That softly sing a lethal rune
Where reeds have caught the fallen moon—
A song more sweet than conium is,
Or honey-blended cannabis,
To draw the dreaming feet of men
On ways where none goes forth again?

Beneath the closely woven grass,
The coiling syrt, more soft and deep
Than some divan where lovers sleep,
Is fain of all who wander there;
And arms that glimmer, vague and bare,
Beckon within the lone morass
Where only dead things dwell and pass.

Beware! the voices float and fall
Half-heard, and haply sweet to thee
As are the runes of memory
And murmurs of a voice foreknown
In days when love dwelt not alone:
Beware! for where the voices call,
Slow waters weave thy charnel pall.

The Nightmare Tarn

I sat beside the moonless tarn alone,
In darkness where a mumbling air was blown—
A moulded air, insufferably fraught
With dust of plundered charnels: there was naught
In this my dream but darkness and the wind,
The blowing dust, the stagnant waters blind,
And sombre boughs of pine or cypress old
Wherefrom a rain of ashes dark and cold
At whiles fell on me, or was driven by
To feed the tongueless tarn; within the sky
The stars were like a failing phosphor wan
In gutted tombs from which the worms have gone.
But though the dust and ashes in one cloud
Blinded and stifled me as might a shroud,
And though the foul putrescent waters gave
Upon my face the fetors of the grave,
Though all was black corruption and despair,
I could not stir, like mandrake rooted there,
And with mine every breath I seemed to raise
The burden of some charnel of old days,
Where, tier on tier, the leaden coffins lie.

While sluggish black eternities went by
I waited; on the darkness of my dream
There fell nor lantern-flame nor lightning-gleam,
Nor gleam of moon or meteor; the wind
Withdrawn as in some sighing tomb, declined,
And all the dust was fallen; the waters drear
Lay still as blood of corpses. Loud and near
The cry of one who drowned in her despair
Came to me from the filthy tarn; the air
Shuddered thereat, and all my heart was grown
A place of fears the nether hell might own,
And prey to monstrous wings and beaks malign:
For, lo! the voice, O dearest love, was thine!
And I—I could not stir: the dreadful weight
Of tomb on ancient tomb accumulate
Lay on my limbs and stifled all my breath,
And when I strove to cry, the dust of death
Had filled my mouth, nor any whisper came
To answer thee, who called upon my name!

The Prophet Speaks

City forbanned by seer and god and devil!
In glory less than Tyre or fabled Ys,
But more than they in mere, surpassing evil!

Yea, black Atlantis, fallen beneath dim seas
For sinful lore and rites to demons done,
Bore not the weight of such iniquities.

Your altars with a primal foulness run,
Where the worm hears the thousand-throated hymn. . . .
And all the sunsets write your malison,

And all the stars unrolled from heaven's rim
Declare the doom which I alone may read
In moving ciphers numberless and dim.

O city consecrate to crime and greed!
O scorner of the Muses' messenger!
Within your heart the hidden maggots breed.

Against your piers the nether seas confer;
Against your towers the typhons in their slumber
In sealed abysms darkly mutter and stir:

They dream the day when earth shall disencumber
Her bosom of your sprawled and beetling piles;
When tides that bore your vessels without number

Shall turn your hills to foam-enshrouded isles,
And, ebbing, leave but slime and desolation,
Ruin and rust, through all your riven miles.

On you shall fall a starker devastation
Than came upon Tuloom and Tarshish old,
In you shall dwell the last abomination.

The dust of all your mansions and the mould
Shall move in changing mounds and clouds disparted
About the wingless air, the footless wold.

The sea, withdrawn from littorals desert-hearted,
Shall leave you to the silence of the sky—
A place fordone, forlorn, unnamed, uncharted,

Where naught molests the sluggish crotali.

The Outer Land

I

From the close valleys of thy love,
Where flowers of white and coral are
And the soft gloom of cave and grove,
How have I wandered, spent and far,
By fell and mountain thence forbanned,
Into this lamia-haunted land?

I could not know the coiling path,
Pebbled with sard and lazuli,
Would lead me to the desert's wrath,
The rancor of the glaring sky,
The tarns that like stirred serpents hiss,
The den of drake and cockatrice.

I roam a limbo long abhorred,
Whose dread horizons flame and flow
Like iron from a furnace poured:
A bournless realm of sterile woe,
Where mad mirages fill the dawn
With roses lost and fountains gone.

O land where dolent monsters mate!
I know the lusts that howl and run
When the red stones reverberate
The red, intolerable sun;
The soot-black lecheries that wail
From Hinnom to the moons of bale.

What desert naiads, amorous,
Have drawn me to their sunken strand!
How many a desert succubus
Has clasped me on her couch of sand!
What liches foul, with breast nor face,
Have seemed to bear thy beauty's grace!

What voices have besought me there
With sweet illusion of thine own,
Luring me, rapt and unaware,
To pits where dying demons moan!
What marble limbs have gleamed as thine—
Slow-sinking into sand or brine!

Briefly, in desert hermitages,
I have lain down in my despair,
Dreaming to sleep as slept the sages:
But unseen lust oppressed the air,
And crimson dreams of incubi,
And thirst of anthropophagi.

II

Entire, from mountains scaled at noon,
I scan the realm of my duress:
Deep-cloven plain and nippled dune,
Like to some sleeping giantess,
Pale and supine, by gods desired
With hearts deliriously fired.

Still without respite, I must follow
Where the faint, exile rills bequeath
Their bitterness to gulf and hollow.
Still the blown dusts of ruin breathe,
Fretting my face. My feet return
By salt-bright shores that blind and burn.

Silence immeasurable creeps
Across my path.... My sharpened ears
Are dinned with tumult from the deeps,
Are frayed by whispers of the spheres;
And darkly, in the sepulchre,
I hear the strident dead confer.

Gnawed by unceasing solitude,
The secret veils of sight grow thin:
High Domes that dazzle and elude,
Columns of darkling god and djinn
Appear; and things forbidden seem
Unsealed as in some awful dream.

My heart, consumed yet unconsuming,
Burns like a dreadful, ardent sun,
The horror of strange nights illuming:
Shall yet I find the ways foregone,
And speak, before the heart of thee,
The still-remembered Sesame?

In Thessaly

When I lay dead in Thessaly,
The land was rife with sorcery:
Fair witches howled to Hecate,
Pouring the blood of rams by night
With many a necromantic rite
To draw me back for their delight....

But I lay dead in Thessaly
With all my lust and wizardry:
Somewhere the Golden Ass went by
To munch the rose and find again
The shape and manlihead of men:
But in my grave I stirred not then,

And the black lote in Thessaly
Its juices dripped unceasingly
Above the rotting mouth of me;
And worm and mould and graveyard must
And roots of cypress, darkly thrust,
Transformed the dead to utter dust.

Le Miroir des blanches fleurs

Remember thou the tarn whose water once allured us
In happy mornings,
See thou the tarn, encinct with mountain bushes,
Where the whiteness of the tiny flowers was mirrored
In a green depth darkened by the shadow of the fire.

It was a faery place, a place enchanted
By the charms of olden time;
Here one had thought to see, from the elfin wood,
From the forest of romaunts, a queen emerge
Mounted on a pale palfray with mirific trappings.

The lofty rocks afar, the lofty trees nearby,
The silence of the waters
And the dark silence weighing down the branches,
All seemed as if brought over from far spaces
Endrowsed by a white spell in the time of ballads.

Oh! in what chronicle, oh! in what legend
Long hidden from our age,
Was this place haply pictured? . . . Flowers of the little shore,
Have you not bloomed about the old-world waters?
How are you transported to this new latitude? . . .

We lingered there, in our souls the sentiment
Of other times, of other scenes:
The charm so potent was, and magical,
That an elfin king, coming full valorously,
Had not surprised our hearts with his sweet horn.

—And thou, in whose loved eye the landscape was redoubled,
Of what high and stately dame
Hast thou borne for a little while the legendary pallor?

And of what troubadour, far-roaming in the boscage,
Have I known the love, the songs, and the chimera?

The Moonlight Desert

Above the desert's dark-obscured expanse
The rounded moon uplooms; at once laid clear
The waste leaps on the sight, the far and near
Known equally. As in a silver trance,
Its sand agleam, the desert lies outrolled.
How bright, seen through the burnt-out atmosphere,
The moon and the augmented stars appear,
Yet how aloof, incurious and cold!

Silent as they the waste outspreads, in white
Unbroken, save where lonely boulders cast
Their dusky-purple shadows on the sand—
Holding Death's terror and its wisdom fast
Within that silence—sinister and bright,
A dead, unutterably ancient land.

Ougabalys

In billow-lost Poseidonis
I was the god Ougabalys:
My three horns were of similor
Above my double diadem,
My one eye was a moon-wan gem
Found in a monstrous meteor.

Incredible far peoples came,
Called by the thunders of my fame,
And fleetly passed my terraced throne,
Where titan pards and lions stood,
As pours a never-lapsing flood
Before the wind of winter blown.

Before me, many a chorister
Made offering of alien myrrh,
And copper-bearded sailors brought,
From isles of ever-foaming seas,

Enormous lumps of ambergris
And corals intricately wrought.

Below my glooming architraves,
One brown eternal file of slaves
Came in from mines of chalcedon,
And camels from the long plateaux
Laid down their sard and peridoz,
Their incense and their cinnamon.

But now, within my sunken walls,
The slow blind ocean-serpent crawls,
And sea-worms are my ministers;
And wondering fishes pass me now,
Or press before mine eyeless brow
As once the thronging worshipers.

Desert Dweller

There is no room in any town (he said)
To house the towering hugeness of my dream.
It straitens me to sleep in any bed

Whose foot is nearer than the night's extreme.
There is too much of solitude in crowds
For one who has been where constellations teem,

Where boulders meet with boulders, and the clouds
And hills convene; who has talked at evening
With mountains clad in many-colored shrouds.

Men pity me for the scant gold I bring:
Unguessed within my heart the solar glare
On monstrous gems that lit my journeying.

They deem the desert flowerless and bare,
Who have not seen above their heads unfold
The vast, inverted lotus of blue air;

Nor know what Hanging Gardens I behold
With half-shut eyes between the earth and moon
In topless iridescent tiers unrolled.

For them, the planted fields, their veriest boon;

For me, the verdure of inviolate grass
In far mirages vanishing at noon.

For them, the mellowed strings, the strident brass,
The cry of love, the clangor of great horns,
The thunder-burdened ways where thousands pass.

For me, the silence welling from dark urns,
From fountains past the utmost world and sun . . .
To overflow some day the desert bourns . . .

And take the sounding cities one by one.

Amithaine

Who has seen the towers of Amithaine
Swan-throated rising from the main
Whose tides to some remoter moon
Flow in a fadeless afternoon? . . .
Who has seen the towers of Amithaine
Shall sleep, and dream of them again.

On falcon banners never furled,
Beyond the marches of the world,
They blazon forth the heraldries
Of dream-established sovereignties
Whose princes wage immortal wars
For beauty with the bale-red stars.

Amid the courts of Amithaine
The broken iris rears again
Restored from gardens youth has known;
And strains from ruinous viols flown
The legends tell in Amithaine
Of her that is its chatelaine.

Dreamer, beware! in her wild eyes
Full many a sunken sunset lies,
And gazing, you shall find perchance
The fallen kingdoms of romance,
And past the bourns of north and south
Follow the roses of her mouth.

The trumpets blare in Amithaine
For paladins that once again
Ride forth to ghostly, glamorous wars
Against the doom-preparing stars.
Dreamer, awake! . . . but I remain
To ride with them in Amithaine.

The Dark Chateau

The mysteries of your former dust,
Your lives declined from solar light—
These would you know, or these surmise?
Beneath a swathed and mummied sun,
Descend where dayless dials rust,
Where the void hourglass fills with night;
And seeing with still-living eyes
Dim Acherontic rivers run,

Follow where shrouded barges float
And fall, in regions of the dead,
Into the sable-foaming depths.
Then over ghostland mountains go
To find, beyond a bridgeless moat,
What stairs with shadows carpeted
Crumble behind the climber's steps
In some foreknown forlorn chateau.

Where exile ghosts of gales that blew
At eve from vintages antique
Still stir the blurring tapestries,
And empty armor guards the rooms
By rotting portraits that were you,
Pass on. From airless cupboards bleak
Startle memorial spiceries
And plagues adrowse in attared glooms.

By oriels charged with stifled stains,
With night-blent purples, gules embrowned,
And spring's lost verdure, graver now
Than cypress at the set of day,
Pause, and look forth: no ghost remains

Save you to gaze on that dim ground
Where once the budding almond-bough
Waved, and the oleander-spray.

Hoar silence is the seneschal
Of court and keep, of niche and coigne.
With drumless ear no lute annoys,
Nor clang from jarring jambarts drawn,
Death, with dulled arrasses for pall,
Waits whitely there; and none will join
Your quest, nor ever any voice
Speak from the chambered epochs gone:

Till from the vaults with shadows brimmed
Shall come a cowled lampadephore,
Holding his lamp, by no breath blown,
To mirrors moony-clear and still
Where never living face is limned,
But wan reflections fixed of yore—
Long-mouldered shapes that were your own—
Graven in glass, unchanged and chill.

Averoigne

In Averoigne the enchantress weaves
Weird spells that call a changeling sun,
Or hale the moon of Hecate
Down to the ivy-hooded towers.
At evening, from her nightshade bowers,
The bidden vipers creep, to be
The envoys of her malison;
And philtres drained from tomb-fat leaves
Drip through her silver sieves.

In Averoigne swart phantoms flown
From pestilent moat and stagnant lake
Glide through the garish festival
In torch-lit cities far from time.
Whether for death or birth, the chime
Of changeless bells equivocal
Clangs forth, while carven satyrs make

With mouths of sullen, sombre stone
Unending silent moan.

In Averoigne abides the mage.
So deep the silence of his cell,
He hears the termless monarchies
That walk with thunder-echoing shoon
In iron castles past the moon—
Fast-moated with eternities;
And hears the shrewish laughters swell
Of Norns the plot the impested age
And wars that suns shall wage.

In Averoigne the lamia sings
To lyres restored from tombs antique,
And lets her coiling tresses fall
Before a necromantic glass.
She sees her vein-drawn lovers pass,
Faintly they cry to her, and all
The bale they find, the bliss they seek,
Is echoed in the tarnished strings
That tell archaic things.

Zothique

He who has trod the shadows of Zothique
And looked upon the coal-red sun oblique,
Henceforth returns to no anterior land,
But haunts a latter coast
Where cities crumble in the black sea-sand
And dead gods drink the brine.

He who has known the gardens of Zothique
Where bleed the fruits torn by the simorgh's beak,
Savors no fruit of greener hemispheres:
In arbors uttermost,
In sunset cycles of the sombering years,
He sips an amaranth wine.

He who has loved the wild girls of Zothique
Shall not come back a gentler love to seek,
Nor know the vampire's from the lover's kiss:

For him the scarlet ghost
Of Lilith from time's last necropolis
Rears amorous and malign.

He who has sailed in galleys of Zothique
And seen the looming of strange spire and peak,
Must face again the sorcerer-sent typhoon,
And take the steerer's post
On far-poured oceans by the shifted moon
Or the re-shapen Sign.

IV. Said the Dreamer

The Castle of Dreams

It lies beyond the farthest sea,
This castle whereunto I flee
When life and time hang wearily.
Yet though so far, 'tis strangely nigh:
Within the breathing of a sigh
One gains the walls secure and high
Of the Castle of Dreams.

Divinely beautiful and great,
Of pearl each dome and tower, and gate,
It stands, a hold of kingly state.
There gyving Time and Space are not,
And cares of Life are all forgot.
No breath of restless change is brought
To the Castle of Dreams.

I walk each wondrous court and hall,
Their varied treasures mine at call,
For there I am the lord of all.
If gold and gems of land and sea,
And broad estates were offered me,
I would not take them for the key
Of the Castle of Dreams.

The Dream-God's Realm

I wandered down Sleep's vast and sunless vale,
Where silence and Cimmerian darkness lay
That never moon nor stars disturb, nor Day
With sword of golden light. Beside the trail
I groping followed, through that secret dale,

A deep and voiceless river stole its way—
Dark Lethe's stream, owning whose opiate sway
I onward went without a doubt or fail.

Till, lo! the atramental veil of night
That, stifling, hung about, behind, before,
Was sudden parted by some unseen hand,
And on my vision leapt a marvelous sight—
A green and joyous plain, with fair skies o'er,
The Dream-God's sunlight-drenched, enchanted land.

Imagination

Imagination, to thine occult sight,
All things are crystal—earth, and sea, and sky,
The seen and the unseen, but limpid light;
Unvisioned stars shall not thy wings defy;
For thee the Future hath no secrecy:
Not with the senses dost thou share the chains
Of Time, and Space's prison; thou dost fly
At will the narrow bourne of their domains
For realms where never bruit of Time and Space attains.

All earth is empire of thy tireless quest:
Thy wings achieve the cloud-invested height,
Or down the distant sunset-flooded West,
Thou vanishest in long unerring flight,
That far outspeeds the swarthy plumes of Night.
Thou findest rest a space on sunset sands,
But soon a star, with Westward-sinking light,
Doth speak of more remote, untrodden strands,
And forth thou farest toward those undiscovered lands.

No realm nor place is secret from thy gaze.
The kingdoms of the bird and fish are thine:
Thy pinions try the eagle's lucid ways,
Then sink to search the foaming vasts of brine.
Thou soar'st to meet the morning's lucent shine,
Where Night and Day beneath thy feet are spread
In long insuperable battle-line;
Then in a breath thou front'st the sunset's red,
Or seekest midnight's realm of mystery and dread.

The ocean yields its secrets unto thee:
Far down beneath the agitated wave,
Where winds stir not the anger of the sea,
Thou plungest to some Nereid's emerald cave,
Whose floors the varied shells of ocean pave.
Here wealth of pearls and strange sea-flowers is thine,
But soon, aweary grown, thy soul doth crave
The noontide air, and where the breakers shine,
Thou soar'st to watch their furious cliff-assailing line.

And then thou questest dusks obscure and strange—
Perpetual twilights—in some jungle's heart,
Where darkness comes, a scarcely-noted change.
Here trees inweave, as if with conscious art,
O'er pools that of the gloom appear a part,
Nor know the silver kiss of star or moon;
And birds strange-plumaged, unauthentic, dart
Through shadows that affirm and then impugn
And leaves and flowers unfamiliar to the noon.

Now o'er a Winter land thou hoverest,
Its sunlit snow to mark, on transient wing.
To trees, in glittering icy armour dressed,
Mild Southern winds bear bruit of coming Spring,
And seek to rouse, with amorous whispering,
The white-robed grass; the clouds austere and grey
That late were earth's dark-vaulted covering,
In ranks disordered, dim, now flee away,
And skies of azure threaten Winter's waning sway.

Thy pinions find a desert drear, forlorn,
Where purple Night fills all the fruitless land,
Deepest a little ere the East of morn
Grows ominous. Her all-deleting hand
Seems promise that her reign awhile shall stand,
When Day, with baleful Cyclopean eye,
Upleaps in flame, and of his sway the sand
Grows ostent, swift. In gardens of the sky,
At his fell breath, the stars are withered utterly!

Of other worlds thy wings ambitious are:
O'er airless gulfs that yawn past reach of Day—
Unfathomed voids of space 'twixt star and star,

The Last Oblivion

Unhesitatingly thou dost essay
Some world exclusive from the sun's wide sway.
Strange forms of life thine eyes thereon descry—
New, unfamiliar—that yet tread a way,
Which, dim and difficult, like ours doth lie
Through dark and pain, toward goals that gleam in unity.

The outer barriers of our system past,
Thou stayst thy flight, to mark in awe and dread,
Some world that ruins down the darkling vast,
Or suns and asteroids, that hurtling red,
To cataclysmic vortices are fed,
And equallized in ruin. Then in gloom
Of planets derelict, long ages dead,
That whirl where never suns nor stars illume,
Thou 'light'st a space to muse upon their frozen doom.

Thy magic spells recall the Past to life,
Before thine eyes the pageant of the years
Doth move, with its reanimated strife,
Its record of forgotten hopes and fears;
Dead loves and hates, and buried joys, and tears
Long-fallen, to thy voice obedient,
Arise and live again; unto thine ears
Voices for ages still are eloquent,
And thou beholdest forms long years in darkness pent.

Once more the might of Rome and Babylon
Lies as a shadow over East and West;
Again Greece sheds a glory as of dawn,
Whose lambent splendour all the years attest;
Once more in empire's tidal, quick unrest,
Egypt and Tyre and Persia rise in state,
And Alexander's world-lust is addressed
Unto their humbling; thrones and nations great
Again are raised or levelled, as the Fates dictate.

'Mong peoples and through realms restored to light,
At will thou wanderest. Thou dost behold
Swart Egypt's gods, enthroned in templed might
Along the Nile, and 'fore thine eyes unfold
Their vanished pomps, with glare of gems and gold;

Thou look'st on Rome, when at its utmost height,
Her grandeur dazzled earth; the wars of old
Upflame and rage anew within thy sight,
With sanguine pageant of advance, retreat, and fight.

The Last Night

I dreamed a dream: I stood upon a height,
A mountain's utmost eminence of snow.
Beholding ashen plains outflung below
To a far sea-horizon, dim and white.
Beneath the spectral sun's expiring light
The world lay shrouded in a deathly glow;
Its last fear-laden voice, a wind, came low;
The distant sea lay hushed, as with affright.

I watched, until the pale and flickering sun,
In agony and fierce despair, flamed high,
And shadow-slain, went out upon the gloom.
Then Night, that war of gulf-born Titans won,
Impended for a breath on wings of doom,
And through the air fell like a falling sky.

Shadow of Nightmare

What gulf-ascended hand is this, that grips
My spirit as with chains, and from the sound
And light of dreamland, draws me to the bound
Where darkness waits with wide, expectant lips?
Albeit thereat my footing holds, nor slips,
The night-born menace and the fear confound
All days and hours of gladness, girt around
With sense of near, unswervable eclipse.

So lies a land whose noon is plagued with whirr
Of bats, than their own shadows swarthier,
That trace their passing upon white abodes,
Wherein from court to court, from room to room,
In hieroglyphics of abhorrent doom,
Is trailed the slime of slowly crawling toads.

A Song of Dreams

A voice came to me from the night, and said,
What profit hast thou in thy dreaming
Of the years that are set
And the years yet unrisen?
Hast thou found them tillable lands?
Is there fruit that thou canst pluck therein,
Or any harvest to be mown?
Shalt thou dig for gold in the mines of the past,
Or trade for merchandise
In the years where all is desolate?
Are they a sea that will bring thee to any shore,
Or a desert that vergeth upon aught but the waste?
Shalt thou drink from the springs that are emptied,
Or find sustenance in shadows?
What value hath the future given thee?
Is there aught in the days yet dark
That thou canst hold with thy hands?
Are they a fortress
That will afford thee protection
Against the swords of the world?
Is there justice in them
To balance the world's inequity,
Or benefit to outweigh its loss?

Then spake I in answer, saying,
Of my dreams I have made a road,
And my soul goeth out thereon
To that unto which no eye has opened,
Nor ear become keen to hearken:
To the glories that are shut past all access
Of the keys of sense;
Whose walls are hidden by the air,
And whose doors are concealed with clarity.
And the road is travelled of secret things,
Coming to me from afar;
Of bodiless powers,
And beauties without color or form
Holden by any loveliness seen of earth.
And of my dreams I have builded an inn

Wherein these are as guests.
And unto it come the dead
For a little rest and refuge
From the hollowness of the unharvestable wind,
And the burden of too great space.

The fields of the past are not void to me,
Who harvest with the scythe of thought;
Nor the orchards of future years unfruitful
To the hands of visionings.
I have retrieved from the darkness
The years and the things that were lost,
And they are held in the light of my dreams
With the spirits of years unborn
And of things yet bodiless.
As in an hospitable house,
They shall live while the dreams abide.

The Dream-Bridge

All drear and barren seemed the hours,
That passed rain-swept and tempest-blown.
The dead leaves fell like brownish notes
Within the rain's grey monotone.

There came a lapse between the showers;
The clouds grew rich with sunset gleams;
Then o'er the sky a rainbow sprang—
A bridge unto the Land of Dreams.

Said the Dreamer

My dreams were nests of horror, whimsey-wrought
With orts and shreds from old abysses brought;
Were eyries built by condor-wingèd awe,
Enskied on somber pinnacles of thought.

Fantastical, I saw the visions shift
Like bubbles that a Titan's breath might lift,
Drowning in seas more deep than his despair—
Iron-colored, soon to shatter or to drift;

Or like illumined crystals fallen from hands
Of gods, that cloud interiorly with lands
Of wider spheres exalted past the sun,
Or burst while thought in idle question stands.

Conscious of gulfs in which I dared not gaze,
I passed on faltering and imperilled ways,
Through lands where hoary mountains danced and roared
To baleful pygmies piping hellish lays.

The flames that wait against the end of things
Were light and limit to my wanderings.
Through deserts bleaching like the bones of death
Aback I fled, and faltered on spent wings

In night Cimmerian, thronged with sorceries,
Where lightnings flamed on empty sands and seas;
Or feared the leopard-crouch of pallid shapes
In Saracenic arches of black trees.

Then in the dream I dreamt that Time was done:
Light still endured, whose touch I might not shun,
Though at my back I heard the lips of Night
Puff out the flaring flambeau of the sun.

I leaned from some black precipice, to see
The pits beneath. One came, not far from me,
Who hurled therein the sockets of the stars
And shell of worlds that rattled emptily.

Dolor of Dreams

The shadow of a sorrow haunts the light,
And sense of dreamt, forgotten tragedy—
Surviving phantom of a memory
Slain by the dawn with shades of yesternight.

Like the blue pallor of the daylight moon,
Most clearly seen within the enshadowed stream,
The wan waste face of some dead, tragic dream
Peers from the twilight places of the noon.

Till, half-bemazed, I am as one who stands
Upon the summit of a misty hill,

And hears remote, one moment loud or still,
The dolor in the bells of blinded lands.

Luna Aeternalis

By an alien dream despatched and driven
In a land to strange stars given,
Stars that summoned forth the moon,
Singing a strange red eldritch rune,
I heard the coming of the moon
With tremulous rim that clomb and rang,
Whose rondure on the horizon rang
A gong distinct with silvern clang,
Re-echoing distantly, until,
Arisen soon,
In silent silver stood the moon
Above the horizon ringing still.

Half-waned and hollow was her brow,
And caverned by the night; but now
Her twilight turned the stars' loud rune
To muted music in a swoon,
Her low light lulled the stars to drowse,
Flicker and fail, and vaguely rouse:
I felt the silence come and go
As the red stars muttered low. . . .

Old with moonlight lay the night,
And on the desert lay
Ancient and unending light
That assured not of the day;
For the half-moon stood to stay
Fixed at the heavens' height
And eternal ere the day.

Triumphant stood the moon
In a false and cold and constant noon:
Surely in conflict fell
The true, lost sun of noon;
The golden might of Uriel
Met some white demon of the moon.

By an alien dream despatched and driven,
I found a land to demons given,
To silvern, silent demons given
That flew and fluttered from out the moon,
Weaving about her tomb-white face
With mop and mow and mad grimace,
And circling down from the semilune
In a serpentine and sinister dance,
To pirouette and pause and prance,
To withdraw and advance,
All in a wan eternal dance.

Echo of Memnon

I wandered ere the dream was done
Where over Nilus' nenuphars,
With all its ears of quivering stars,
The darkness listened for the sun.

Ere shadows were, ere night was gone,
I found the one whom suns had sought,
And waiting at his feet, methought
Had speech with Memnon in the dawn. . . .

Sad as the last, lamenting star
He sang, and clear as morning's gold:
Unto his voice I saw unfold
The hesitant, pale nenuphar.

But dolorous like the peal of dooms,
And proclamation of the night,
The waste returned that voice of light
With echo from its hollow tombs!

Nightmare

As though a thousand vampires, from the day
Fleeing unseen, oppressed that nightly deep,
The straitening and darkened skies of sleep
Closed on the dreamland dale in which I lay.

Eternal tensions numbed the wings of time
While through unending narrow ways I sought
Awakening; up precipitous gloom I thought
To reach the dawn, far-pinnacled sublime.

Rejected at the closen gates of light
I turned, and down new dreams and shadows fled,
Where beetling shapes of veiled, colossal dread
With Gothic wings enormous arched the night.

The Last Goddess

(A Fragment)

To laud the loves of old,
I sought for splendors fabulous and far:
The curls of one were black Circean petals
Of poppies blown by night
In the sad gardens of a sinful star;
Her eyes were mystic metals,
Wrought with a secret told
By lost archangels in their flight
To women of the worlds that stray
On the red verges of the nether day;
Her voice was like a lulling music blown
At sunset from an isle of spells
Across a lake of rosy nenuphar;
And yet therein
Betimes I caught the chill and crystal bells
That grieved, and grieved alone,
Above the fallen din
Of cities drowsed with revelry and sin.

Love Malevolent

I fain would love thee, but thy lips are fed
With poison-honey, hivèd in a skull;
They seem like scarlet poppies, beautiful
For delving roots, deep-clenchèd in the dead.

Thine eyes are coloured like the nightshade-flow'r. . . .
Blent in the opiate perfume of thy breath
Are dreams, and purple sleep, and scented death
For him that is thy lover for an hour.

Mandragora, within the graveyard grown,
Hath given thee its carnal root to eat,
And vipers, born and nurstled in a tomb,

From fawning mouths drip venom at thy feet;
Yet from thy lethal lips and thine alone,
Love would I drink, as dew from poison-bloom.

The Wingless Archangels

Beyond the bourn of dreams, their fortunate sphere,
Golden and large in some rich galaxy,
Rolls upon ways prolonged of harmony;
And they, with wingless toil of many a year,
Unto the calm of heavens have clomb anear—
Wise with the secrets of eternity,
And forcing truce with time. . . . They deem them free
From change, and from the old, unchanging fear.

But on their immortality is blight—
Whose dream betraying deserts have undone:
They turn, where winds make chill the ashen light,
Blown as from space and bleak oblivion;
And mark the dim, portentous breath of Night,
A mist penumbral on the noontide sun.

Enchanted Mirrors

These are enchanted mirrors that I bring,
By demons wrought from metals of the moon
To burnished forms of lune or plenilune:
Therein are faery faces vanishing,
And warm Pompeiian phantoms lovelier
Than mortal flesh or marble; and the gleam
Of suns that from Saturnia rose in dream
And sank on golden worlds that never were.

Therein you shall behold unshapen dooms,
And ghoul-astounding shadows of the tombs;
Oblivion, with eyes like poppy-buds,
Or love, with blossoms plucked in Devachan,
In stillness of the santal-pillared woods;
But nevermore the moiling world of man.

Selenique

Perfect, marmoreal, curved and carven statue-wise,
Your hard immaculate beauty dulls the sharpness of desire,
And chills it to a changeless passion—
A frozen passion bright and pallid,
And clear as is the ghostly fervor of the moon's white fire.
And all the dreams of you are lunar dreams—
Such bright and hueless visions as are born
Of moonset on autumnal meres forlorn,
Where the white lotus lingers,
Unstirred with full and fragile petals overblown
That the least wave would loosen
And shatter like the touch of fingers;
While the high clouds upon the western hills,
Immobile, rest like towering palaces
And mausoleums wrought of dim fantastic stone.

Maya

Fools of the world, who dream that dreams are true—
Believing still that life is what it seems,
And trustful that the world is more than dreams—
Free for a little, I have laughed at you:
Knowing all this a ghostly gossamer
In some eternal room of darkness spun;
A laughter of forgotten gods that were,
Echoing still in waste oblivion.

But once again, as others, I have lent
Myself to earthly ways and earthly walls:
Illusion of illusion, fantasy
Of doubtful phantoms, nevermore to be

When slumber on the last delirium falls
And lulls the tossing shadows turbulent.

Fantaisie d'Antan

Lost and alien lie the leas,
Purfled all with euphrasies,
Where the lunar unicorn
Breasts an amber-pouring morn
Risen from hesperian seas
Of a main that has no bourn.
Only things impossible
There in deathless glamor dwell:
Pegasus and sagittary,
Trotting, part the ferns of faery,
Succubi and seraphim
Tryst among the cedars dim;
Where the beaded waters brim,
White limoniads arise,
Interlacing arms and tresses
With the sun-dark satyresses;
There, on Aquilonian skies,
Gryphons, questing to and fro
For the gold of long ago,
Find at eve an aureate star
In the gulf crepuscular;
There the Hyperboreans,
Pale with wisdom more than man's,
Tell the wileful centauresses
Half their holocryptic lore;
There, at noon, the tritonesses,
All bemused with mandragore,
Mate with satyrs of the shore.
Love, could we have only found
The forgotten road that runs
Under all the sunken suns
To that time-estrangèd ground,
Surely, love were proven there
More than long and lone despair;
Holden and felicitous,

Love were fortunate to us;
And we too might ever dwell,
Deathless and impossible,
In those amber-litten leas,
Circled all with euphrasies.

In Slumber

The stench of stagnant waters broke my dream,
Wherethrough had run, with living murmur and gleam,
The Rivers four of the Earthly Paradise:
From the azured flame of those effulgent skies
And valleys lifting censers of vast bloom,
I was drawn down into a deathlier gloom
Than lies on Styx's fountain. By such light
As shows the newly damned their dolorous plight,
I trod the shuddering soil of that demesne
Whence larvae swarmed, malignant and obscene,
Like writhen mists from some Maremma reeking:
Through the gross air, fell incubi went seeking
Their prey that slumbered helpless; at my knee
There clung the python-bodied succubi;
I heard the wail of them that walked apart,
Each with a suckling vampire at his heart;
And, as I stumbled loathly on, the ground
Was rent with noiseless thunder all around
To pits that teemed with direr prodigies:
Grey, headless coils, and worm-shaped infamies
Unmeasured, rose above the sun that rotted
Black as a corpse in heavens thick and clotted;
The rusty clang and shaken soot of wings
Deafened and stifled me; from pestilent springs
Slime-mantled horrors boiled with fume and hiss
To plunge in frothing fury down the abyss.
Then, from an outmost circle of that hell,
The tumbling harpies came, detestable,
With beaks that in long tatters tore my breast
And wove from these their crimson, wattled nest.

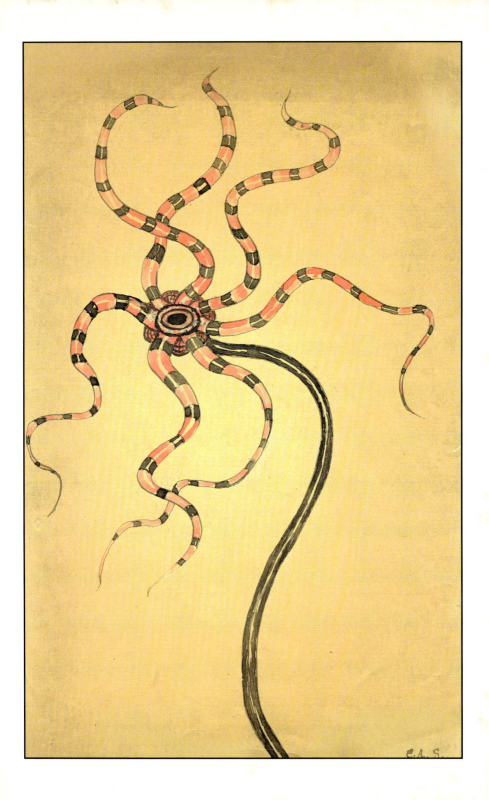

V. The Refuge of Beauty

The Power of Eld

Beneath my dome of sleep, secure-immersed
And filled of peace, such blinded power of scath
As Samson once employed, was loosed in wrath,
And tumult with tempestuous arm dispersed
The pillared silence: came a wind accurst,
That, shuddering, as from hidden peril fled—
A sign; and then the Past's uncharneled dread
In swarming visions on the darkness burst.

Betrayed by Sleep unto the might of Eld,
I knew the terror of its kings, the fear
Of thrones abased by some resistless flood;
Howlings of prophets mingled in mine ear
With death-lament of cities, far-beheld
'Neath drenching flame that made the night as blood.

Strangeness

O love, thy lips are bright and cold,
Like jewels carven curiously
To symbols of a mystery,
A secret lost ere time was old.

Like woven amber, finely spun,
Thy hair, enwoofed with golden light,
Remembers yet the flaming flight
Of some unknown archaic sun.

Thine eyes are crystals green and chill,
Wherein, as in a shifting sea,
Wan fires and drowning lusters flee
To starless deeps for ever still.

Fallen across thy dreaming face,
The dawn is made a secret thing,
Like flame of crimson lamps that swing
In midnight caverns dim with space.

Sphinx-like, unsolved eternally,
Thy beauty's riddle doth abide,
And love hath come, and love hath died,
Striving to read the mystery.

The Nereid

Her face the sinking stars desire:
Unto her place the slow deeps bring
Shadow of errant winds that wing
O'er sterile gulfs of foam and fire.

Her beauty is the light of pearls.
All stars and dreams and sunsets die
To make the fluctuant glooms that lie
Around her; and low noonlight swirls

Down ocean's firmamental deep
To weave for her who glimmers there
Elusive visions, vague and fair;
And night is as a dreamless sleep:

She has not known the night's unrest
Nor the white curse of clearer day;
The tremors of the tempest play
Like slow delight about her breast.

The berylline pallors of her face
Illume the kingdom of the drowned.
In her the love that none has found,
The unflowering rapture, folded grace,

Await some lover strayed and lone,
Some god misled, who shall not come
Though the decrescent seas lie dumb
And sunken in their wells of stone.

But nevermore of him, perchance,
Her enigmatic musings are,

Whose purpling tresses float afar
In grottoes of the last romance.

Serene, an immanence of fire,
She dwells for ever, ocean-thralled,
Soul of the sea's vast emerald.
Her face the sinking stars desire.

Exotique

Thy mouth is like a crimson orchid-flower
Whence perfume and whence poison rise unseen
To moons aswim in iris or in green,
Or mix with morning in an eastern bower.

Thou shouldst have known, in amaranthine isles,
The sunsets hued like fire of frankincense,
And noontides fraught with far-borne redolence,
The mingled spicery of purple miles.

Thy breasts, where blood and molten marble flow,
Thy warm white limbs, thy loins of tropic snow—
These, these, by which desire is grown divine,

Were made for dreams in mystic palaces,
For love and sleep and slow voluptuousness,
And summer seas afoam like foaming wine.

Transcendence

To look on love with disenamored eyes;
To see with gaze relentless, rendered clear
Of hope or hatred, of desire and fear,
The insuperable nullity that lies
Behind the veils of various disguise
Which life or death may haply weave; to hear
Forevermore in flute and harp the mere
And all-resolving silence; recognize
The gules of autumn in the greening leaf,
And in the poppy-pod the poppy-flower:—
This is to be the lord of love and grief,
O'er time's illusion and thyself supreme,

As, half-aroused in some nocturnal hour,
The dreamer knows and dominates his dream.

The Tears of Lilith

O lovely demon, half-divine!
Hemlock and hydromel and gall,
Honey and aconite and wine
Mingle to make that mouth of thine—

Thy mouth I love: but most of all
It is thy tears that I desire—
Thy tears, like fountain-drops that fall
In gardens red, Satanical;

Or like the tears of mist and fire,
Wept by the moon, that wizards use
To secret runes when they require
Some silver philter, sweet and dire.

Cleopatra

Thy beauty is the warmth and languor of an orient autumn,
Caressing all the senses—
With light from skies of heavy azure,
With perfume from blossoms large as thuribles,
That hang in the berylline dusk of palms;
With the balmy kiss of wind and wave beneath Canopus;
And the songs of exotic birds
That pass in vermilion-flashing flight from isle to isle
On an ocean of lazuli.
O, sweetness in the inmost sense,
As of blood-red fruits that have grown by the waters of Lethe,
Or fragrance of purple lilies crushed in a cypress-grove
By the sleeping limbs of Eros! . . .
Thou pervadest me with thy love
As the dawn pervadeth a valley among mountains,
Or as sunset filleth the amaranth-colored sea;
The desire of thy heart is upon me
Like a summer wind from Cythera,
Where Venus lies among the tiger-lilies

By a pool whose waters are fed from secret springs;
I inhale thy love
As the breath of hidden gardens of purple and scarlet,
Where Circe trails a gown
Whose colors are the reddening gold of flame
And the azure of the skies of autumn.

The Refuge of Beauty

From regions of the sun's half-dreamt decay,
All day the cruel rain strikes darkly down;
And from the night thy fatal stars shall frown—
Beauty, wilt thou abide this night and day?

Roofless, at portals dark and desperate,
Wilt thou a shelter unrefused implore,
And past the tomb's too-hospitable door
Evade thy lover in eluding Hate?

Alas, for what have I to offer thee?—
Chill halls of mind, dank rooms of memory
Where thou shalt dwell with woes and thoughts infirm;

This rumor-throngèd citadel of Sense,
Trembling before some nameless imminence;
And fellow-guestship with the glutless Worm.

Sandalwood

Upon thy separate road
(Thou, who hast chosen the world's appointed way)
My songs shall be as the perfume of sandalwood
Borne by a secret wind from form-lost irretrievable islands,
Where the hibiscus bowers of our love,
And the palaces of roseate marble,
With all their vine-caught pillars,
Were dreamt, but never builded.
And through the clanging tumult of thy days,
A rumour of phantom chords,
Of dulcimers destroyed,
And lutes that might have been,

Shall call and cry to thee as the burden of my songs;
And thou shalt hear the spectral fountains fall,
Delicious as the laughter
Of ghosts of amorous women,
Of flowers that never were;
And winds that flee, exiguous and faint,
Like the sighs of long-dead lovers,
Through seedless gardens without place or name.
And thou shalt know
What immaterial myrtles, pale and sweet
As the breasts of love-worn queens,
Or flushed as with a maiden's glowing blood,
Were strewn to make
The forfeit couch where two shall never come;
And know
What topaz or what Tyrian-coloured wines
The palm-entrellised grapes
Withhold in lost Cocaigne.

The Last Oblivion

Not while the woods are redolent with spring,
Or scentless immortelles of autumn blow,
Shall I evade your loveliness, or know
Surcease of love and love's remembering.

But haply wandering, worlds and cycles hence,
Through unforeseen fantastic avatars,
I shall forget you in the future stars,
And take of time an alien recompense.

Till in some strange and latter planet, wrought
From molten shards and meteor-dust of this,
My hand shall pluck an unsuspected bloom

That lifts again the scarlet of your kiss;
And I shall muse and loiter, knowing not
The love that perished like a lost perfume.

Alienage

Dear one, what do we here?
Petal by petal falls the alien spring
In gardens where we pass ungarlanded,
And seek once more the doves and myrtles dead
In some retrieveless year;
And claim no leaf or blossom for our own. . . .
O Paphos, and the moons of Paphos flown!
My golden dove, canst thou recall
Nights when delight was all,
And high desire could still outlive the dawn?
Hast thou forgot,
Here, in the grey, sad world that knows us not,
The years when we were nymph and centaur, drawn
To elder forests deep
That spring had turned to chrysolite and gold?
Hast thou forgot the tale of kisses told
By summer waters calm as sleep,
When Hesperèan sunsets touched thy hair
From islands lost and fair?

Dear one, what do we here?
Beyond the window-pane
The shifting veils of rain
Bedim the bitter world that is not ours;
And on dishevelled flowers
There falls a hueless twilight, brief and drear. . . .
Give me thy lips again—
Let us forget the weariness and pain,
And the supreme disaster of our birth,
While in thy flesh my lingering
Slow kisses move and cling
And love alone hath verity or worth.
Ah, let me find, about thy bosom's fruit,
The fragile, vague perfume
Of unseen lilies crushed within the gloom
Of forests lone and old;
Ah, let me seek in leisured long pursuit
Amid thy harvest-colored hair,
For suns and summers of remembered gold;

And seal my lips on throat and bosom fair,
Till where my kisses fell, the phantom rose
Of Paphos blows.

Adventure

Let us leave the hateful town
With its stale, forgotten lies;
Far beneath renewing skies,
Where the piny slope goes down,
All with April love and laughter—
None to leer and none to frown—
We shall pass and follow after
Shattered lace of waters spun
On a steep and stony loom
Down the depths of laurel-gloom.
Finding there a world re-made
In the fern-embowered shade,
Weaving bright oblivion
Still from frailest blossom-trove,
We shall mix our wilding love
With the woodland and the sun.

Let us loiter, hand in hand,
Hearing but the heart's command,
Half our steps by kisses stayed,
Prove the spring-enchanted glade;
Breast to breast and limb to limb,
Seize our happiness and bind it—
Lose the pulse of time and find it,
Free as vagrant seraphim.
Ever leave regret and rue
To the dutiful and jealous
Fools that are not near to tell us
All the things we should not do.

Though the bedded ferns be broken,
And dishevelled blossoms lie
On the rumpled moss for token
Of the day's mad errantry—
Still the tacit pines will keep

Darkly in their sighing sleep
All the sweet and perilous story;
And the oaks and willows hoary
For unheeding ears will tell
Only things ineffable;
And the later eyes that look
On the pool-delaying brook,
Shall not see within its glass
Two that came to kiss and pass.

Interrogation

Love, will you look with me
Upon the phosphor-litten labor of the worm—
Time's minister, who toils for his appointed term,
And has for fee
All superannuate loves, and all the loves to be?

Love, can you see, as I,
The corpses, ghosts and demons mingled with the crowd?
The djinns that men have freed, grown turbulent and proud?
Alastor, Asmodai?
And all-unheeded envoys from the stars on high?

Know you the gulfs below,
Where darkling Erebus on Erebus is driven
Between the molecules—atom from atom riven,
And tossing to and fro,
Incessant, like the souls on Dante's wind of woe?

Know you the deeps above?
The terror and vertigo of those who gaze too long
Upon the crystal skies unclouded? Are you strong
With me to prove
Even in thought or dream the dreadful pits above?

Know you the gulfs within?
The larvae, the minotaurs of labyrinths undared?
The somber foam of seas by cryptic sirens shared?
The pestilence and sin
Borne by the flapping shroud of liches met within?

Canticle

In my heart a wizard book,
Only love shall ever look:
Darling, when thou readest there,
Wisely falter and forbear
Ere thou turn'st the pages olden,
Deeply writ and deeply folden,
Where the legends of lost moons
Lie in chill unchanging runes.
Trifle not with charm or spell,
Heptagram or pentacle,
Leave in silence, long unsaid,
All the words that wake the dead.

Darling, in my heart withholden,
Letters rubrical and golden
Tell the secret of our love
And the philtred spells thereof;
There, my memories of thee,
Half of all the gramarie,
Are a firm unfading lore:
Read but these . . . and read no more. . . .
Shall it profit thee to find
Loves that went with snow and wind?
Leave in silence, long unsaid,
All the words that wake the dead.

To Antares

Antares, star of memory,
Her name I whisper unto thee;
Be thou tonight my messenger
And featly bear my love to her,
When she, as I, with like desire,
Gazes upon thy sanguine fire,
Dreaming of all thou sawest of old,
Things not to be forgot or told,
And borne beyond all others' knowing
By tongueless Lethe in its flowing:

Till, gazing thus, in one same thought
Our hearts shall be together brought,
And each insuperable mile
Forfeit its triumph, for awhile.

Connaissance

Only through the senses have I known you,
But you are nearer than the things of sense—
Nearer than is the daylight in mine eyes,
And nearer
Than scent of orchard blossoms in the dark,
Or touch of mountain wind or water flowing,
Or long belovèd music heard once more
Among belovèd faces.
The sense of you is more than sight or audience,
The thought of you lies deeper
Than the clear springs of recollection,
The shallow tarns of dreaming.
You flow a stronger blood within my blood,
Poured from a heart whose pulses
Suffuse the veins of centaurs and of gods.
You are a thought encompassing all other thoughts,
Even as the sea enfolds the kelp and coral
And the sea-flowers and sea-monsters
And the domes of deep unsunned Atlantis.

Exorcism

Like ghosts returning stealthily
From those grey lands
Palled with funereal ashes falling
After the burnt-out sunset,
The mists of the valley reach with wavering, slow,
Malignant arms from pine to pine, and climb the hill
As fatal memories climb
To assail some heart benighted and bewitched. . . .

And once they would have crept
Around me in resistless long beleaguerment,

To lay their death-bleak fingers on my heart:
But now
My memories are of you and of the many graces
And tender, immortal, mad beatitudes of love;
And every chill and death-born phantom,
Made harmless now and dim,
Must pass to haunt the inane, unpassioned air;
And only living ghosts
Of raptures gone or ecstasies to be,
May touch me and attain within the circle
Your arms have set about me.

Lamia

Out of the desert lair the lamia came,
A lovely serpent shaped as women are.
Meeting me there, she haled me by the name

Belovèd lips had used in days afar;
And when the lamia sang, it seemed I heard
The voice of love in some old avatar.

Her lethal beauty like a philtre stirred
Through all my blood and filled my heart with light:
I wedded her with ardor undeterred

By the strange mottlings of her body white,
By the things that crept across us in her den
And the dead who lay beside us through the night.

Colder her flesh than serpents of the fen,
Yet on her breast I lost mine ancient woe
And found the joy forbid to living men.

But, ah, it was a thousand years ago
I took the lovely lamia for bride . . .
And nevermore shall they that meet me know

It is a thousand years since I have died.

Farewell to Eros

Lord of the many pangs, the single ecstasy!
From all my rose-red temple builded in thy name,
Pass dawnward with no blasphemies of praise or blame,
No whine of suppliant or moan of psaltery.

Not now the weary god deserts the worshipper,
The worshipper the god . . . but in some cryptic room
A tocsin tells with arras-deadened tones of doom
That hour which veils the shrine and stills the chorister.

Others will make libation, chant thy litanies. . . .
But, when the glamored moons on inmost Stygia glare
And quenchlessly the demon-calling altars flare,
I shall go forth to madder gods and mysteries.

And through Zothique and primal Thule wandering,
A pilgrim to the shrines where elder Shadows dwell,
Perhaps I shall behold such lusters visible
As turn to ash the living opal of thy wing.

Haply those islands where the sunsets sink in rest
Will yield, O Love, the slumber that thou hast not given;
Or the broad-bosomed flowers of some vermilion heaven
Will make my senses fail as on no mortal breast.

Perchance the wind, on Aquilonian marches blowing
From the low mountains isled in seas of russet grass,
Will make among the reeds a sweeter shuddering pass
Than tremors through the chorded flesh of women flowing.

Perchance the fountains of the dolorous rivers four
In Dis, will quench the thirst thy wine assuages never;
And in my veins will mount a twice-infuriate fever
When the black, burning noons upon Cimmeria pour.

Yea, in those ultimate lands that will outlast the Earth,
Being but dream and fable, myth and fantasy,
I shall forget . . . or some image reared of thee,
Dreadful and radiant, far from death, remote from birth.

Some Blind Eidolon

Longer ago than Eden's oldest morn,
Ere beast or man was born,
I chose for mine
The love whereto some ancient evil clings,
With sombre spectra barring still the wings
That wear the irised flame of suns divine—
The love whereto some ancient evil clings.

Down all the planet-paven ways of time,
Lengthening from the prime
A shadow falls—
A thing that climbs the pharos-guarded gates,
Or by the wizard's dying brazier waits,
Or lairs amid the many-tapered halls—
A thing that climbs the pharos-guarded gates.

Have we not known, O witch, O queen, O maid,
The stain that creeps unstayed
In love's alloy?
The fretful moth that frays the bed of lust?
The wingless and unweariable disgust
That overtakes the philtre-goaded joy—
The fretful moth that frays the bed of lust?

Though proud as gardened Babylon our bliss,
Mortal corruption is
The seed self-sown
Amid the rampant flowers and the founts. . . .
The laughter of some blind eidolon mounts
Where the self-deluded mourner sobs alone
Amid the ruined flowers and the founts.

Dark loves of all the vanished avatars,
What candor-heated stars,
What crimson hells,
Consumed us long ago but cleansed us not,
Nor could absolve us of the sombre blot!
Yea, all the Moloch-hearted suns and hells
Consumed us long ago but cleansed us not!

Where limbos of unfathomed ice immure,
Shall yet we couch secure

Our sundered clay?
What sea wherein the unshapen planets sleep
Shall make us one in its potential deep—
Washing the lethal dross of self away—
What sea wherein the unshapen planets sleep?

Bacchante

Men say the gods have flown;
The Golden Age is but a fading story,
And Greece was transitory:
Yet on this hill hesperian we have known
The ancient madness and the ancient glory.

Under the thyrse upholden,
We have felt the thrilling presence of the god,
And you, Bacchante, shod
With moonfire, and with moonfire all enfolden,
Have danced upon the mystery-haunted sod.

With every autumn blossom,
And with the brown and verdant leaves of vine,
We have filled your hair divine;
From the cupped hollow of your delicious bosom,
We have drunk wine, Bacchante, purple wine.

About us now the night
Grows mystical with gleams and shadows cast
By moons for ever past;
And in your steps, O dancer of our delight,
Wild phantoms move, invisible and fast.

Behind, before us sweep
Maenad and Bassarid in spectral rout
With many an unheard shout;
Cithaeron looms with every festal steep
Over this hill resolved to dream and doubt.

What Power flows through us,
And makes the old delirium mount amain,
And brims each ardent vein
With passion and with rapture perilous?
Dancer, of whom our votive hearts are fain,

You are that magic urn
Wherefrom is poured the pagan gramarie;
Until, accordantly,
Within our bardic blood and spirit burn
The dreams and fevers of antiquity.

Resurrection

Sorceress and sorcerer,
Risen from the sepulcher,
From the deep, unhallowed ground,
We have found and we have bound
Each the other, as before,
With the fatal spells of yore,
With Sabbatic sign, and word
That Thessalian moons have heard.

Sorcerer and sorceress,
Hold we still our heathenness—
Loving without sin or shame—
As in years of stake and flame.
Share we now the witches' madness,
Wake the Hecatean gladness,
Call the demon named Delight
From his lair of burning night.

Love that was, and love to be,
Dwell within this wizardry:
Lay your arm my head beneath
As upon some nighted heath
Where we slumbered all alone
When the Sabbat's rout was flown;
Let me drink your dulcet breath
As in evenings after death.

Witch belovèd from of old,
When upon Atlantis rolled
All the dire and wrathful deep,
You had kissed mine eyes asleep.
On my lids shall fall your lips
In the final sun's eclipse;

And your hand shall take my hand
In the last and utmost land.

The Sorcerer to His Love

Within your arms I will forget
The horror that Zimimar brings
Between his vast and vampire wings
From out his frozen oubliette.

The terror born of ultimate space
That gnaws with icy fang and fell,
The sucklings of the hag of hell,
Shall flee the enchantment of your face.

Ah, more than all my wizard art
The circle our delight has drawn:
What evil phantoms thence have gone,
What dreadful presences depart!

Your arms are white, your arms are warm
To hold me from the haunted air,
And you alone are firm and fair
Amid the darkly whirling storm.

The Hill of Dionysus

This is enchanted ground
Whereto the nymphs are bound;
Where the hoar oaks maintain,
While seasons mount or wane,
Their ghostly satyrs, dim and undispelled.
It is a place fulfilled and circled round
With fabled years and presences of Eld.

These things have been before,
And these are things forevermore to be;
And he and I and she,
Inseparate as of yore,
Are celebrants of some old mystery.

Under the warm blue skies
The flickering butterflies,
Dancing with their frail shadows, poise and pass.
Now, with the earth for board,
The bread is eaten and the wine is poured;
While she, the twice-adored,
Between us lies on the pale autumn grass.

Thus has she lain before,
And thus we two have watched her reverently;
More beautiful, and more
Mysterious for her body's nudity.

Full-burdened with the culminating year,
The heavens and earth are mute;
Till on a fitful wind we seem to hear
Some fainting murmur of a broken flute.
Adown the hillside steep and sere
The laurels bear their ancient leaves and fruit.

These things have happened even thus of yore,
These things are part of all futurity;
And she and I and he,
Returning as before,
Participate in some unfinished mystery.

Her hair, between my shoulder and the sun,
Is turned to iridescent fire and gold:
A witch's web, whereon
Wild memories are spun,
And magical delight and sleep unfold
Beyond the world where Anteros is lord.

It is the hour of mystical accord,
Or respite, and release
From all that hampers us, from all that frets,
And from the vanity of all regrets.
Where grape and laurel twine,
Once more we drink the Dionysian wine,
Ringed with the last horizon that is Greece.

Midnight Beach

In starlight, by the ghostly sea,
We ran, we loitered, hand in hand,
Along the lone, unending strand;
Where, flowing in the surf-wet sand,
The wan stars raced or paused as we.

Aloof we seemed, from time and change,
Like runes a magian might unroll
Upon some old unfading scroll,
Or phantoms loosed from earthly dole
In starry freedom, lone and strange.

Some great, unspoken gramarie
Had exorcised that incubus,
The world, that fell away from us. . . .
Reborn, and dear, and perilous,
The past arose beside the sea.

Returning in that mystic hour,
Above us hovered many a night
That had your eyes alone for light:
Full-petaled, past all worldly blight,
Love bloomed an amaranthine flower.

In starlight, by the ghostly sea,
I caught and kissed you as of yore;
We ran, we tarried, as before;
Where, flowing on the surf-wet shore,
The wan stars raced or paused as we.

Omniety

I am the master of strange spells
Whereby the past is made tomorrow,
And April blows in fields long fallow,
And Dis unseals Hyblaean wells.

From out the house of incarnation
I pass with ether or with air,
In climes and times of otherwhere
Resume my destiny and station.

Loosed from the coils of space and number,
I am the shadowy self who stands
Kissing your lips, holding your hands,
Warding your labor and your slumber.

Dream not to escape me, day or night,
Even in the passionate arms of others,
For I am one with all your lovers,
Sharing their pain and their delight.

VI. TO THE DARKNESS

Ode on Imagination

Imagination's eyes
Outreach and distance far
The vision of the greatest star
That measures instantaneously—
Enisled therein as in a sea—
Its cincture of the system-laden skies.
Abysses closed about with night
A tribute yield
To her retardless sight;
And Matter's walls reveal the candent ores
Rock-held in furnaces of planet-cores.
She penetrates the sun's transplendent shield,
And through that inner vastness, sphered and dire,
Pierces his dreadful heart, whose gurge of fire
Heaves outward, riven by Titanic throes,
And fills his frame with tide and cataract
Of thunder-pulsing, incandescent streams.
Her eyes exact
From the Moon-Sphinx that wanes and grows
In wastes celestial, alien dreams
Brought down on wings of spectral beams.
Adown the clefts of under-space,
She rides, her steed a falling star,
To seek, where void and vagueness are,
Some mark or certainty of place.
Upon their heavenly precipice,
The gathered suns shrink back aghast
From that interminate abyss,
And threat of sightless anarchs vast.

She stands endued
With supermundane crown, and vestitures
Of emperies that include

All underworlds and overworlds of dream—
Domains with shadow bound,
Cimmerian and profound,
And heights of some Himalaya supreme
Where moon-transcending light endures.
She roams in grey, fantasmal lands, where grow
In scarce-discernèd fields and closes blind,
Faint blossoms stirred by wings of eidolons;
Or wanders all bemused and slow
In woods where only nameless echoes go
And wraiths of ancient wind:
In twilight there she shuns
The strident day, while ecstasy and grief
Speak only in vague whispers like the leaf.

Upon some supersensual eminence
She hears the fragments of a thunder loud,
Where lightnings of ulterior Truth intense
Flame through the walls of hollow cloud.
But these she may not wholly grasp
With unsupernal clasp.
Her eyes inevitably see,
'Neath rounds and changes of exterior things,
The movements of Essentiality—
Of ageless principles—that alter not
To temporal alterings—
Unswerved by shattered worlds upbuilt once more,
And stars no longer hot;
Or broken constellations strewn
Like coals about the heavenly floor,
And rush of night upon the noon
Of their lost worlds, unsphered retrievelessly
In icy deserts of the sky.
From the beginning of the spheres,
When systems nebulous out-thrown
Drove back the brinks
Of nullity with limitary marks,
Till end of suns and sunless death of years,
To her are known
The unevident inseparable links
That bind all deeps, all suns, all days and darks.

Retrospect and Forecast

Turn round, O Life, and know with eyes aghast
The breast that fed thee—Death, disguiseless, stern:
Even now, within my mouth, from tomb and urn,
The dust is sweet. All nurture that thou hast
Was once as thou, and fed with lips made fast
On Death, whose sateless mouth it fed in turn.
Kingdoms abased, and Thrones that starward yearn,
All are but ghouls that batten on the past.

Monstrous and dread, must it forever abide,
This inescapable alternity?
Must beauty blossom, rooted in decay,
And night devour its flaming hues alway?
Sickening, will Life not turn eventually,
Or ravenous Death at last be satisfied?

To the Darkness

Thou hast taken the light of many suns,
And they are sealed in the prison-house of gloom.
Even as candle-flames
Hast thou taken the souls of men
With winds from out a hollow place;
They are hid in the abyss as in a sea,
And the gulfs are over them,
As the weight of many mountains,
As the depth of many seas;
Thy shields are between them and the light;
They are past its burden and bitterness;
The spears of the day shall not touch them,
The chains of the sun shall not hale them forth.

Many men there were,
In the days that are now of thy realm,
That thou hast sealed with the seal of many deeps;
Their feet were as eagles' wings in the quest of Truth—
Aye, mightily they desired her face,
Hunting her through the lands of life
As men in the blankness of the waste

That seek for a buried treasure-house of kings.
But against them were the veils
That hands may not rend nor sabers pierce;
And Truth was withheld from them
As a water that is seen afar at dawn,
And at noon is lost in the sand
Before the feet of the traveller.
The world was a barrenness,
And the gardens were as the waste.
And they turned them to the adventure of the dark,
To the travelling of the land without roads,
To the sailing of the sea that hath no beacons.
Why have they not returned?
Their quest hath found end in thee,
Or surely they had fared
Once more to the place whence they came,
As men that have journeyed to a fruitless land.
They have looked on thy face,
And to them it is the countenance of Truth.
Thy silence is sweeter to them than the voice of love,
Thine embrace more dear than the clasp of the beloved.
They are fed with the emptiness past the veil,
And their hunger is filled;
They have found the waters of peace,
And are athirst no more.
They know a rest that is deeper than the gulfs,
And whose seal is unbreakable as the seal of the void;
They sleep the sleep of the suns,
And the vast is a garment unto them.

A Dream of Beauty

I dreamed that each most lovely, perfect thing
That Nature hath, of sound and form and hue—
The winds, the grass, the light-concentering dew,
The gleam and swiftness of the sea-bird's wing;
Blueness of sea and sky, and gold of storm
Transmuted by the sunset, and the flame
Of autumn-colored leaves, before me came,
And, meeting, merged to one diviner form.

Incarnate Beauty 'twas, whose spirit thrills
Through glaucous ocean and the greener hills,
And in the cloud-bewildered peaks is pent.
Her face the light of fallen planets wore,
But as I gazed, in doubt and wonderment,
Mine eyes were dazzled, and I saw no more.

The Pursuer

Climbing from out what nadir-fountained sea,
From nether incarnations none may sound—
Sealed with the night of suns, forever bound
With frozen systems—comest thou to me,
Despair, whose darker name in memory
I know not, bringing from the dead profound,
With cerements and sepulchral purples wound,
The foulness of thine immortality?

O shape of loathlier horrors, here untold,
Have I not climbed secure from their abyss,
Those lower spheres, those limbos dire and old?
Thou tearest me beyond the hells of this,
Down chasms dreadful for the light of tears
Where worm-like terror crawls in the undead years!

In the Desert

I met the night in unfamiliar lands,
In realmless desolations, drear and far,
Where no life was, nor any shard remained
Of tomb or cenotaph: all salient things
Long since had fed the prone monotony
Of the null forgetful sands. Here darkness came
Directly as a king who mounts the throne
Of some Cimmerian primogeniture.
A waif of day, I wandered beneath stars
That seemed the unnumbered steely eyes of Death
Seeking the lost necropoles.

                A wind
Rose loudly on the middle night, and passed,

Laden with nameless, immemorial dust,
The shapeless ghost of empires. In that dark
Alien and secret as the heart of death,
I knew not if the wind, remembering
Walls that were great upon its ancient way,
Sang now their threnody, or if the dust,
Tongueless itself, found in the shrilling wind
A tongue for its regret. I, wandering there,
Felt but the dust's unseen, mysterious kiss,
Heard but the grievous wind. . . . So have I known
Lost visions vaguely grasp at memory
And fall back unrecalled. . . . Then, laden still
With sorrow and with dustiness of Eld,
Stirring the desert dark, the wind went on
To leave its dwindling burden at the feet
Of splendid morning unendurable.

The Nameless Wraith

As one who seeks the silver moth of night
Where moonless gardens lose the afterglow,
My soul went forth ineffably, to know
Some vaguer vision unrevealed of light.

From halcyon fells whereon the falcons range,
From Hesper, and the sunsets mountain-born,
And from the trembling freshness of the morn
I turned me to a dreamland still and strange.

It seemed the hueless ashes of the day
And darkened glories filled that glooming world:
The spectrum of hesternal suns was furled
In immemorial valleys vast and grey.

Ruins, and wrecks of many a foundered year,
Doubtfully known, bestrewed the unvisioned verge,
Where, from unsounding reaches of blind surge,
Some nameless wraith of beauty fluttered near.

Was it the dove from shrines of lost delight?
The nightingale from love's necropolis?

What dream-led messenger of time's abyss
Came from the dark, and vanished in the night?

To the Daemon of Sublimity

I wane and weary: come, thou swifter One,
With vans of ether-sundering instancy,
Zoned with essential night and sovereignty
Of flame septuple, strong to blind or stun
Beyond the bolted levin. Though earth, undone,
Fail to thy meteor-fraught epiphany,
Though Time be as a chasm-riven sea,
Come thou, and bear me to thy chosen sun.

Yea, in the fiery fastness of the star
That thine empyreal wings most often find,
Thy lordliest eyrie, lone in gulf and gloom,
Leave me and lose me, safe from wasting war
Of finite things unworthy, and resigned
To some apotheosis of bright doom.

Desolation

It seems to me that I have lived alone—
Alone, as one that liveth in a dream:
As light on coldest marble, or the gleam
Of moons eternal on a land of stone,
The days have been to me. I have but known
The silence of Thulean lands extreme—
A silence all-attending and supreme
As is the sea's enormous monotone.

Upon the waste no palmed mirages are,
But strange chimeras roam the steely light,
And cold parhelia hang on hill and scaur
Where flowers of frost alone have bloomed. . . . I crave
The friendly clasp of finite arms, to save
My spirit from the ravening Infinite.

Inferno

Grey hells, or hells aglow with hot and scarlet flowers;
White hells of light and clamor; hells the abomination
Of breathless, deep, sepulchral desolation
Oppresses ever—I have known them all, through hours
Tedious as dead eternity; where timeless powers,
Leagued in malign, omnipotent persuasion—
Wearing the guise of love, despair and aspiration,
For ever drove through ashen fields and burning bowers

My soul that found no sanctuary.... For Lucifer,
And all the weary, proud, imperious, baffled ones
Made in his image, hell is anywhere: the ice
Of hyperboreal deserts, or the blowing spice
In winds from off Sumatra, for each wanderer
Preserves the jealous flame of sad, infernal suns.

Dissonance

The harsh, brief sob of broken horns; the sound
Of hammers, on some clanging sepulcher;
Lutes in a thunder-storm; a dulcimer
By sudden drums and clamoring bugles drowned;
Crackle of pearls, and gritting rubies, ground
Beneath an iron heel; the heavy whirr
Of battle-wheels; a hungry leopard's purr;
And sigh of swords withdrawing from the wound:—

All, all are in thy dreadful fugue, O life,
Thy dark, malign and monstrous music, spun
In hell, from a delirious Satan's dream! . . .
O! dissonance primordial and supreme—
The moan, the thunder, evermore at strife,
Beneath the unheeding silence of the sun!

Remembered Light

The years are a falling of snow,
Slow but without cessation,

On hills and mountains and flowers and worlds that were;
But snow, and the crawling night wherein it fell,
May be washed away in one swifter hour of flame:
Thus it was that some slant of sunset
In the chasms of pilèd cloud—
Transient mountains that made a new horizon,
Uplifting the west to fantastic pinnacles—
Smote warm in a buried realm of the spirit,
Till the snows of forgetfulness were gone.
Clear in the vistas of memory,
The peaks of a world long unremembered
Soared further than clouds but fell not,
Based on hills that shook not nor melted
With that burden enormous, hardly to be believed.
Rent with stupendous chasms,
Full of an umber twilight,
I beheld that larger world:
Bright was the twilight, clear like ethereal wine
Above, but low in the clefts it thickened,
Dull as with duskier tincture.
Like whimsical wings outspread but unstirring,
Flowers that seemed spirits of the twilight
That must pass with its passing—
Too fragile for day or for darkness—
Fed the dusk with more delicate hues than its own;
Stars that were nearer, more radiant than ours,
Quivered and pulsed in the clear thin gold of the sky.

These things I beheld
Till the gold was shaken with flight
Of fantastical wings like broken shadows
Forerunning the darkness;
Till the twilight shivered with outcry of eldritch voices
Like pain's last cry ere oblivion.

The Incubus of Time

Ill days and dolorous nights and years accurst—
The increase of evil, that is twin to life;
Weariness of re-animated strife,

And love, renewing with the selfsame thirst
The same delight—a drunken Tantalus;
And the thousand-chorded monotones of pain
Irresolubly played and played again
On broken souls and bodies ruinous.

I would the world and all its leaden woe,
Its ennui, like incumbent tombs of stone,
And time's each minute, as an iron clod,
Were bound about the monstrous throat of God,
And He were drawn in deathless overthrow
To some blind nadir of the voids unknown.

Laus Mortis

The imperishable phantoms, Love and Fame,
Nor Beauty, burning on the mist and mire
A fugitive uncapturable fire,
Nor God, that is a darkness and a name—
Not these, not these my choric dreams acclaim,
But Death, the last and ultimate desire,
Great Death I praise with litany and lyre
And somber prayer implacably the same.

O, incommunicable hope that lies
Deep in despair, as tapers that illume
Some fearful fane's arcanic, sacred gloom!
O, solace of all weary hearts and wise!—
The dream which Satan hath for anodyne,
Which is to God a sweet and secret wine.

The Hope of the Infinite

My hope is in the unharvestable deep
That shows with eve the treasure of the stars
To mournful kings behind their palace-bars,
And wanderers outworn, and boys who weep
A shattered bauble—or above the sleep
Of headsmen, and of men condemned to die,
Pours out the moon's white mercy from on high,
Or hides with clement gloom the hours that creep

Like death-worms to the grave.... And I have ta'en
From stormy seas by sunset glorified,
Or from the dawn of ashen wastes and wide,
Some light re-gathered from the lamps that wane,
And promise of a translunary Spain
Where loves forgone and forfeit dreams abide.

Antepast

The thought of death to me
Is like a well in some oasis dim—
Cool-gleaming, hushed, and hidden gratefully
Among the palms asleep
At silver evening on the desert's rim.

Or as a couch of stone,
Whereon, by moonlight, in a marble room,
Some fevered king reposes all alone—
So is the hope of sleep,
The inalienable surety of the tomb.

Forgotten Sorrow

A stranger grief than any grief by music told
Is mine: regret for unremembered loves, and faces
Veiled by the night of some unknown farewell, or places
Lost in the dusty ebb and lapse of kingdoms old
On the slow desert, rises vague and manifold
Within my heart at summer twilight. Through the spaces
Of all oblivion, voidly then my soul retraces
Her dead lives given to the marbles and the mould
In dim Palmyra, or some pink, enormous city
Whose falling columns now the boles of mightier trees
Support in far Siam.... All grievous love, and pity,
All loveliness unheld for long, and long estranged,
Appeals with voices, indistinguishably changed,
Like bells in deep Atlantis, tolled by summer seas.

Lunar Mystery

O'er gardens lulled with ghostly light
In music leaned the languorous moon,
The burden of the murmured night.

Where amaranthine lilies wore,
In lofty pallor fully blown,
An ivory silence evermore,

Bemused, I saw the night's white song,
The flowers' moon-measured lullaby,
Its visible pale rune prolong.

Then, to my spelled, reluctant ear,
A whisper louder than the light
Pierced as from alien presence near;

Till half I deemed to shortly see
A silver seraph of the moon,
Or star-shape harping mystery.

But wingless yet the midnight seemed,
The garden footless to my gaze,
Save for a wind that briefly gleamed

Upon the pensive-pacèd hours,
And moonlight fluttering like a moth
Amid the swayed, enormous flowers.

The Funeral Urn

My heart is like some onyx urn
Upon whose cold and carven side
Antique symbolic serpents glide
In scrolls that wander and return;

Where orchid and where columbine
Intort their blooms ambiguously;
Where over some exotic tree
Clambers the grape's familiar vine.

How fair and strange the art thereof!
But—irony supreme—within,

The poisonous black dust of sin
And ashes from dark pyres of love.

Mors

Sweeter the thought of death to me
Than love's own sleep or any dream;
Than starlight on some ebon stream
Or moonlight on the marble sea.

Like black and mummia-laden wine
My soul foredrains oblivion:
The bitter splendors of the sun
Resolved in Lethe's anodyne.

Love and desire and dead delight
And dead despair are shades that pass
As in a necromancer's glass
To mingle with the shades of night.

They pass. . . . The secret peace I crave
Like a black shroud enwraps me round—
Lost, and voluptuously drowned
In the dark languor of the grave.

September

Slumberously burns the sun
Over slopes adust and dun,
Leaning southward through September. . . .
I forget and I remember,
Life is half oblivion. . . .
Somnolently burns the sun.

Close and dim the horizons creep,
Earthward lapse the heavens in sleep;
Woodlands faint with azure air
Seem but bourns of Otherwhere:
Swooning with ensorcelled sleep,
Close and dim the horizons creep.

Embers from a dreamland hearth,
Glow the leaves in croft and garth;
Vines within the willows drawn
Relume the gold of visions gone;
Darkly burn, in croft and garth,
Embers from a dreamland hearth.

Sleepy like an airless fire,
Smoulders my supreme desire:
Throeless, in the tranquil sun,
Hearts could melt and merge as one
In forgetful soft desire
Drowsy like an airless fire.

Ennui

Thou art immured in some sad garden sown with dust
Of fruit of Sodom that bedims the summer ground,
And burdenously bows the lilies many-crowned,
Or fills the pale and ebon mouths of sleepy lust
The poppies raise. And, falling there imponderously,
Dull ashes emptied from the urns of all the dead
Have stilled the fountain and have sealed the fountain-head
And pall-wise draped the pine and flowering myrtle-tree.

Thou art becalmed upon the slothful ancient main
Where Styx and Lethe fall; where skies of stagnant grey
With the grey stagnant waters meet and merge as one:
How tardily thy torpid heart remembers pain,
And love itself, as aureate islands far away
On seas refulgent with the incredible red sun.

VII. The Sorcerer Departs

To Omar Khayyam

Omar, within thy scented garden-close,
When passed with eventide
The starward incense of the waning rose—
Too precious to abide
After the glad and golden death of spring—
Omar, thou heardest then,
Above the world of men,
The mournful rumor of an iron wing,
The sough and sigh of desolating years,
Whereof the wind is as the winds that blow
Out of a lonesome land of night and snow
Where timeless winter weeps with frozen tears;
And in thy bodeful ears
The brief and tiny lisp
Of petals curled and crisp,
Fallen at eve in Persia's mellow clime,
Was mingled with the mighty sound of time.

Omar, thou knewest well
How the fair days are sorrowful and strange
With time's inexorable mystery
And terror ineluctable of change:
Upon thine eyes the bleak and bitter spell
Of vision, thou didst see,
As in a magic glass,
The moulded mists and painted shadows pass—
The ghostly pomps we name reality;
And, lo, the level field,
With broken fane and throne
And dust of old, unfabled cities sown,
In unremembering years was made to yield,

From out the shards of Power,
The pillars frail and small
That lift for capital
The blood-like bubble of the poppy-flower;
And crowns were crumbled for the airy gold
The crocus and the daffodil should hold
As inalienable dower.
Before thy gaze the sad unvaried green
The cypresses like robes funereal wear,
Was woven on the gradual looms of air
From threadbare silk and tattered sendaline
That clothed some ancient queen;
And from the spoilt vermilion of her mouth
The myrtles rose, and from her ruined hair
And eyes that held the summer's ardent drouth
In blown, disrooted bowers;
And amber limbs and breast
Through ancient nights by sleepless love oppressed,
Or by the iron flight of loveless hours.

Knowing the weary wisdom of the years,
The empty truth of tears;
The suns of June that with some great excess
Of ardor slay the unabiding rose;
And grey-haired winter, wan and fervorless,
For whom no flower grows;
Seeing the paradisal bloom that pales
On orient snows untrod
In magic morns that grant,
Across a land of common green and grey,
The disenchanted day;
Knowing the gulf-deep veils
And walls of adamant
That ward the darkling verities of God—
Knowing these things, ah, surely thou wert wise
To kiss on ardent breast and avid mouth
Some girl whose eyes
Were golden with the sun-belovèd south—
To pluck the rose and drain the rose-red wine
In gardens half-divine;
Before the broken cup

Be filled and covered up
In dusty seas of everlasting drouth.

To Nora May French

Importunate, the lion-throated sea,
Blind with the mounting foam of winter, mourns
To cliffs where cling the wrenched and labored roots
Or cypresses, and blossoms granite-grown
Lose in the gale their tattered petals, cast
On bleak, tumultuous cauldrons of the tide
Where fell thine ashes. Past the cobalt bay
The morning dunes a dust of marble seem—
Wrought from primeval fanes to Beauty reared,
And shattered by some vandal Titan's mace
To more than time's own ruin. Woods of pine
Above the dunes in Gothic gloom recede,
And climb the ridge that arches to the north
Long as a lolling dragon's chine. The gulls,
Like ashen leaves far off upon the wind,
Flutter above the broad and smouldering sea
That lightens with the fire-white foam. But thou,
Of whom the sea is urn and sepulcher,
Who hast thereof a blown tumultuous sleep
And stormy peace in gulfs impacable—
What carest thou if Beauty loiter there,
Clad with the crystal noon? What carest thou
If sharp and sudden balsams of the pine
Mingle for her in the air's bright thurible
With keener fragrance proffered by the deep
From riven gulfs resounding? . . . Knowest thou
What solemn shores of crocus-colored light,
Reared by the sunset in its realm of change,
Will mock the dream-lost isles that sirens ward,
And charm the icy emerald of the seas
To unabiding iris? Knowest thou
The waxing of the wan December foam—
A thunder-cloven veil that climbs and falls
Upon the cliffs forevermore?

                              Thou art still
As they that sleep in the eldest pyramid—
Or mounded with Mesopotamia
And immemorial deserts! Thou hast part
In the wordless, dumb conspiracy of death—
Silence wherein the warrior kings accord
And all the wrangling seers! If now thy voice
In any wise return, and word of thee,
It is a lost, incognizable sigh
Upon the wind's oblivious woe, or blown,
Antiphonal, from wave to plangent wave,
In the vast unhuman sorrow of the main
On tides that lave the city-laden shores
Of lands wherein the eternal vanities
Are served at many altars; tides that wash
Lemuria's unfathomable walls,
And idly sway the weed-involvèd oars
Rotting amid the moles of orichalchum
In deep Atlantis; tides resurgent ever
From coral-coffered bones of all the drowned,
And sunless tombs of pearl that krakens guard.

II

As none shall roam the sad Leucadian rock
Above the sea's immitigable moan,
But in his heart a song that Sappho sang,
And flame-like murmur of the muted lyres
That time has not extinguished, and the cry
Of nightingales two thousand years ago
Shall mix with those remorseful chords that break
To endless foam and thunder; and he learn
The unsleeping woe that lives in Mytelene
Till wave and deep are dumb with ice, and rime
Has paled the rose for ever—even thus,
Daughter of Sappho, passion-souled and fair,
Whose face the lutes of Lesbos would have sung
And white Erinna followed—even thus
The western wave is eloquent of thee,
And half the wine-like fragrance of the foam
Is attar of thy spirit, and the pines,

From breasts of darkling, melancholy green,
Release remembered echoes of thy song
To airs importunate. No wraith of fog,
Twice-ghostly with the Hecatean moon,
Nor rack of blown, phantasmal spume shall rise,
But I will dream thy spirit walks the sea,
Unpacified with Lethe. Thou art grown
A part of all sad beauty, and my soul
Has found thy buried sorrow in its own,
Inseparable for ever. Moons that pass
Immaculate, to solemn pyres of snow,
And meres whereon the broken lotus dies,
Are kin to thee, as wine-lipped autumn is,
With suns of swift irreparable change,
And lucid evenings eager-starred. Of thee
The pearlèd fountains tell, and winds that take
In one white swirl the petals of the plum
And leave the branches lonely. Royal blooms
Of the magnolia, pale as beauty's brow,
And foam-white myrtles, and the fiery, bright
Pomegranate-flowers, will subtly speak of thee
While spring has speech and meaning. Music has
Her fugitive and uncommanded chords,
That thrill with tremors of thy mystery,
Or turn the void thy fleeing soul has left
To murmurs inenarrable, that hold
Epiphanies of blind, conceiveless vision,
And things we dare not know, and dare not dream.

(*Note:* Nora May French, one of the most gifted women-poets of America, died by her own hand at Carmel in 1907. Her ashes were strewn into the sea from Point Lobos.)

On Re-reading Baudelaire

Forgetting still what holier lilies bloom
Secure within the garden of lost years,
We water with the fitfulness of tears
Wan myrtles with an acrid sick perfume;
Lethean lotus, laurels of our doom,

Dark amarant with tall unswaying spears,
Await funereal autumn and its fears
In this grey land that sullen suns illume.

Ivy and rose and hellebore we twine.
Voluptuous as love, or keen as grief,
Some fleeing fragrance lures us in the gloom
To Paphian dells or vales of Proserpine. . . .
But all the flowers, with dark or pallid leaf,
Become at last a garland for the tomb.

To George Sterling: A Valediction

I

Farewell, a late farewell! Tearless and unforgetting,
Alone, aloof, I twine
Cypress and golden rose, plucked at the chill sunsetting,
Laurel, amaracus, and dark December vine
Into a garland wove not too unworthily
For thee who seekest now an asphodel divine.
Though immaterial the leaf and blossom be,
Haply they shall outlinger these the seasons bring,
The seasons take, and tell of mortal monody
Through many a mortal spring.

II

Once more, farewell! Naught is to do, naught is to say,
Naught is to sing but sorrow!
For grievous is the night, and dolorous the day
In this one hell of all the damned we wander thorough.
Thou hast departed--and the dog and swine abide,
The fetid-fingered ghouls will delve, on many a morrow
In charnel, urn and grave: the sun shall lantern these,
Oblivious, till they too have faltered and have died,
And are no more than pestilential breath that flees
On air unwalled and wide.

III

Let ape and pig maintain their council and cabal:
In ashes gulfward hurled,

Thou art gone forth with all of loveliness, with all
Of glory long withdrawn from a desertless world.
Now let the loathlier vultures of the soul convene:
They have no wings to follow thee, whose flight is furled
Upon oblivion's nadir, or some lost demesne
Of the pagan dead, vaulted with perfume and with fire,
Where blossoms immarcescible in verspertine
Strange amber air suspire.

IV

Peace, peace! for grief and bitterness avails not ever,
And sorrow wrongs thy sleep:
Better it is to be as thou, who art forever
As part and parcel of the infinite fair deep--
Who dwellest now in mystery, with days hesternal
And time that is not time: we have no need to weep,
For woe may not befall, where thou in ways supernal
Hast found the perfect love that is oblivion,
The poppy-tender lips of her that reigns, eternal,
In realms not of the sun.

V

Peace, peace! Idle is our procrastinating praise,
Hollow the harps of laud;
And not necessitous the half-begrudgèd bays
To thee, whose song forecrowned thee for a lyric god,
Whose name shall linger strangely, in the sunset years,
As music from a more enchanted period—
An echo flown upon the changing hemispheres,
Re-shaped with breath of alien maiden, alien boy,
Re-sung in future cities, mixed with future tears,
And with remoter joy.

VI

From Aphrodite thou hast turned to Proserpine:
No treason hast thou done,
For neither goddess is a goddess more divine,
And verily, my brother, are the twain not one?
We too, as thou, with hushed desire and silent paean,
Beyond the risen dark, beyond the fallen sun,

Shall follow her, whose pallid breasts, on shores Lethean,
Are favorable phares to barges of the world;
And we shall find her there, even as the Cytherean,
In love and slumber furled.

To Howard Phillips Lovecraft

Lover of hills and fields and towns antique,
How hast thou wandered hence
On ways not found before,
Beyond the dawnward spires of Providence?
Hast thou gone forth to seek
Some older bourn than these—
Some Arkham of the prime and central wizardries?
Or, with familiar felidae,
Dost now some new and secret wood explore,
A little past the senses' farther wall—
Where spring and sunset charm the eternal path
From Earth to ether in dimensions nemoral?
Or has the Silver Key
Opened perchance for thee
Wonders and dreams and worlds ulterior?
Hast thou gone home to Ulthar or to Pnath?
Has the high king who reigns in dim Kadath
Called back his courtly, sage ambassador?
Or darkling Cthulhu sent
The sign which makes thee now a councilor
Within that foundered fortress of the deep
Where the Old Ones stir in sleep
Till mighty temblors shake their slumbering continent?

Lo! in this little interim of days
How far thy feet are sped
Upon the fabulous and mooted ways
Where walk the mythic dead!
For us the grief, for us the mystery....
And yet thou art not gone
Nor given wholly unto dream and dust:
For, even upon
This lonely western hill of Averoigne

Thy flesh had never visited,
I meet some wise and sentient wraith of thee,
Some undeparting presence, gracious and august.
More luminous for thee the vernal grass,
More magically dark the Druid stone,
And in the mind thou art forever shown
As in a magic glass;
And from the spirit's page thy runes can never pass.

H. P. L.

Outside the time-dimension, and outside
The ever-changing spheres and shifting spaces—
Though the mad planet and its wrangling races
This moment be destroyed—he shall abide
And on immortal quests and errands ride
In cryptic service to the kings of Pnath,
Herald or spy, on the many-spangled path
With gulfs below, with muffled gods for guide.

Some echo of his voice, some vanished word
Follows the light with equal speed, and spans
The star-set limits of the universe,
Returning and returning, to be heard
When all the present worlds and spheres disperse,
In other Spicas, other Aldebarans.

Soliloquy in a Ebon Tower

The poet speaks, addressing a framed picture of Baudelaire upon a bookcase:

The lamp burns stilly in the standing air,
As in some ventless cavern. Through wide windows
The midnight brings a silence from the stars,
And perfumes that the planet dreams in sleep.
The hounds have ceased to bay; and the cicadas
To ply their goblin harps. The owl that whilom
Hooted his famine to a full-chapped moon,
Has pounced upon his gopher, or has gone
To fresher woods behind a farther hill;

And Hecate has grounded all the witches
For some glade-hidden Sabbat.

                        In my room
The quick, malign, relentless clock ticks on,
Firm as a demon's undecaying pulse,
Or creak or Charon's oak-locks as he plies
Between the shadow-crowded shores. Evoked
Within the vaults of my funereal brain,
Voices awaken, sibilant and restless
Tongues of the viper's charnel-fostered brood,
Half-grown, amid the shreds of winding-sheets
And crumbling wicker of old bones. They sing,
Those little voices, all the poisonous
Importunate melodies you too have heard,
O Baudelaire, in midnights when the moon
Sank, followed by some cloudy hearse of dreams,
Into the skyless nadir of despond.
Black-flickering, cloven tongues! Though we distill
Quintessences of hemlock or nepenthe,
We cannot slay the small, the subtle serpents
Whose mother is the lamia Melancholy
That feeds upon out breath and sucks our veins,
Stifling us with her velvet volumes.

                          Now
My thoughts pursue the santal and sad myrrh
Sighed by the shrouds of all hesternal sorrows.
Busied with old regrets, they carry on
Such commerce as the burrowing necrophores
Conduct from grave to grave; or pause to mumble
Snatches of ancient amorous elegies,
Deploring still some splendid, stately love—
Gone like the pomps of void Ecbatana—
That only lives in epodes, but will rise
To ghost the goldless morrows, clothed about
With hues of suns declining and decayed,
And crowned with ruinous autumn.

                        Other thoughts
Exhume the withered wing-shards of ideals
Brittle and light as perished moths, or bring

To sight the mummied bats of blear mischance,
By dismal eves and moons disastrous flying,
But fallen now, and dead as are the heavens
Their vans have darkened. On belovèd deaths
I muse, and through my twice-wept tears re-gather
The treads that Clotho and Lachesis have spun
And Atropos has cut; and see the bleak
Sinister gleaming of the steely shears
Behind the riven arrasses of time. . . .

What weapon can we arm us with? what bulwark
Build against grief and time? What moat renewed
With waters mortal as those that shroud Gomorrah,
Will the sea-going termite never ferry
To gnaw the ebon tower, the ebon ark
Holding the Muses' covenant? Splendor-brimmed,
What grail of God or Satan will suffice
For all the breadless days, the unguerdoned labors?

Yet, for a toll so light, by Song transported
To sail beyond Elysium and Theleme,
And see, from oblivion looming, balmier shores
Of fables infinite! To light our dreams
At rose Aldebaran or sky-huge Antares,
Then quench their heat, or temper Damascus thought
In cold aphelions and apastrons far!
To pace the sun's Typhoean ramparts vast!
To couch on Saturn's outmost ring, or roll
With Pluto through his orb of eventide
Whose Hesper is the dwindled sun! To flaunt
Before the blind an immarcescible purple
Won from the murex of Uranian seas,
And fire-plucked vermeil of Vulcan, worn against
The aguish mists and wintry shadows! Thus
We triumph; thus the laurel overtops
The upas and the yew; and we decline
No toil, no dolor of our votive doom.

High-housed within the Alchemic Citadel,
We are served by Azoth and by Alkahest.
Out of the gleamless mire and sand we make
Pactolian metal. Fumed from our alembics,

The world dissolves like vapors opium-wrought,
Or drips, condensed, to philtres and to venoms
That Circe nor Simaetha dreamed. We build,
Daedalus-like, a labyrinth of words
Wherein our thoughts are twi-shaped Minotaurs
The ages shall not slay. Our ironies,
Like marbled adders creeping on through time,
Shall fang the brains of poets yet to be.
Our nacred moons and corposants of beauty
Shall float on ever-mootful lands retained
By Lar and Lemur; where Chimera flies,
And still the Sphinx unanswerably rules;
Where the red phantoms we have loosed from Dis
Still haunt the thickets and the cities; where
Our phosphor lamps may serve as well as any
Along the rutted way to Charon's wharf.

Cycles

The sorcerer departs . . . and his high tower is drowned
Slowly by low flat communal seas that level all . . .
While crowding centuries retreat, return and fall
Into the cyclic gulf that girds the cosmos round,
Widening, deepening ever outward without bound . . .
Till the oft-rerisen bells from young Atlantis call;
And again the wizard-mortised tower upbuilds its wall
Above a re-beginning cycle, turret-crowned.

New-born, the mage re-summons stronger spells, and spirits
With dazzling darkness clad about, and fierier flame
Renewed by aeon-curtained slumber. All the powers
Of genii and Solomon the sage inherits;
And there, to blaze with blinding glory the bored hours,
He calls upon Sham-hamphorash, the nameless Name.

Glossary

Nouns are listed in the singular, save where indicated. For present or past participles, look under the main verb.

Acheron: one of the six rivers in the Greek underworld
aconite: a plant whose root is used as a medicine or poison
adamantine: exceptionally hard
aguish: subject to ague (fever marked by chills)
alabraundine: vt. of *alabandine,* a precious stone known to the ancients
Alastor: an avenging deity or spirit in Greek mythology
alastor: an avenging spirit
alembic: an apparatus used for distilling
Algebar: Arabic name for the constellation Orion
Alioth: a name for the star Epsilon Ursae Majoris
almandine: a corruption of *alabandine:* an alumina iron garnet, violet in color
amarant(h): an imaginary flower
amort: dead
anademe: a wreath or garland for the head
anarch: a leader of anarchy
anodyne: anything that relieves pain
Antenora: imaginary realm invented by CAS
antepast: a foretaste
Anteros: son of Aphrodite and Ares, and the brother of Eros; the god of unhappy love
anthropophagus: a man-eater
apastron: the point at which the distance between the two components of a binary star is greatest; the point of closest approach is the periastron
aphelion: a planet's farthest point from the sun in its orbit

appanage: an adjunct
architrave: the molding around a window or doorway
argentry: silver
arras: a kind of tapestry
Asmodai: an evil spirit in the Jewish religion
atomy: a skeleton
atramental: of or pertaining to ink
attar: oil or perfume made from flowers
Baalim: plural of *Baal,* a false god or devil
bale: evil or disaster
barbican: a defensive tower at a gate
Bassarid: a Bacchante
berylline: pertaining to beryl (a mineral used as a gem)
besom: a broom, or anything that sweeps or cleans
blench: to make pale
boscage: a thicket or grove
Brierean: pertaining to Briareus, a hundred-armed giant in Greek mythology
brume: mist or fog
buttle: to pour out a drink
byre: a cow barn
candent: glowing with heat
carnelian: a kind of chalcedony
caryatid: a supporting column in the form of a woman
cate: a delicacy
celadon: a pale shade of green
cerementa: a shroud
cerulean: sky-blue
chalcedony: a type of quartz used for jewelry
chancre: a venereal sore or ulcer
chanticleer: a rooster
chatelaine: the mistress of a castle

chimera: a mythical creature with the head of a lion, the body of a goat, and a tail consisting of a serpent
chine: the backbone
choric: pertaining to a chorus
chrysoberyl: a mineral (beryllium aluminate) sometimes used as a gem
ciclaton: cloth-of-gold
cimar: a robe or loose, light garment
cirque: circle
clepsammia: an instrument for measuring time
clepsydra: an ancient device for measuring time
close: an enclosed garden
Cocaigne: a mythical realm of ease and luxury
cockatrice: an imaginary serpent that has the power to kill by a look
cockodrill: var. of *crocodile*
Cocytus: one of the six rivers in the Greek underworld
coeval: of the same age
coigne: a projecting corner
conium: a plant of the hemlock family
conterminate: having the same boundaries or limits
coronal: a diadem or crown
corposant: St. Elmo's fire (a glowing ball of electrical discharge, as seen on church steeples)
crepitate: to make a crackling sound
crepuscular: pertaining to twilight
cresset: a metal container for burning fuel and used as a torch or lantern
croft: a small enclosed field
crotalus (pl. crotali): a kind of snake
crotalum: a type of castanet
crud: to coagulate
damassin: a type of damask
decrescent: waning
Dis: the ruler of the underworld in Roman mythology
dolent: sad
donjon-keep: the innermost and most fortified section of a castle
dwale: belladonna; deadly nightshade
dynast: a lord or ruler
eidolon: a phantom or image
embrue: to stain
empyreal: pertaining to the heavens

encinct: girdled
enisled: to make an island of
ensorcell: to bewitch
ephemera: a transient object
ephemeris (pl. ephemerides): an astrological almanac
ephemeris: an astronomical almanac
eremite: a hermit
erodent: something that erodes
erst: formerly
euphrasy: a kind of herb
exiguous: scanty
eyne: archaic plural of *eye*
fantasque: fantastic
flaff: to flap or flutter
foison: a plentiful crop or harvest
forbanned: banished
foredone: ruined or destroyed
forefend: to forbid or ward off
foulder: to flash or thunder forth
frory: frozen
fulgor: a brilliant or flashing light
fulvous: tawny
fumitory: a type of plant used as a medicine
garth: an enclosed yard or garden
genius: the presiding spirit of a locale
gier-eagle: a kind of vulture
glistering: shining
gnomon: the pin on a sundial
gnurled: knobbed
gorget: a piece of armor for the throat
gramarie: magic or occult knowledge
gules: the color red
gurge: a whirlpool
gyre: a circular motion
gyve: a shackle
haply: perhaps
hebenon: a poisonous juice
hecatomb: a sacrifice of animals
hesperian: pertaining to the west
hesternal: pertaining to yesterday
Hinnom: a valley near Jerusalem; sometimes used as an alternate name for Gehenna or Hell
holocryptic: indecipherable
horrent: bristling; *figuratively,* frightening
Hyblaean: pertaining to the Sicilian town of Hybla, where honey was produced in antiquity

hydromel: water mixed with honey
immarcesescible: not withering
immitigable: that which cannot be mitigated
immortelle: a flower that keeps its color and shape when dried
impacable: unappeasable
impest: to inflict with the plague
implacable: inexorable
importunate: stubbornly persistent
imprecatory: uttering an imprecation (curse)
incarnadine: to redden or to bloody
incognizable: incapable of being perceived
inenarrable: incapable of being told
interminate: boundless
intervital: existing between two lives
intort: to twist or curl inwards
irremeable: not capable of returning
irrision: derision or mockery
jambart: var. of *jamber* (armor for the legs)
jape: a joke or jest
Kobold: a mischievous elf or gnome (German folklore)
lampadephore: a torch-bearer
leman: a sweetheart or lover
lentor: slowness
levin: a lightning-bolt
liana: a type of woody vine
lich: a corpse
limitary: serving as a boundary
limoniad: a meadow nymph
littoral: an area along the shore
lote: lotus
lune: the moon
lustrum: a period of five years
madreperl: mother-of-pearl
Maenad: a female member of the orgiastic cult of Dionysus
magian: a magician or sorcerer
Malebolge: in Dante's *Divine Comedy*, the eighth circle of Hell
malison: a curse
mandragore: a mandrake (a poisonous plant)
mantichora/martichora: a fabulous creature with a lion's body, a man's head, and a scorpion's tail

Maremma: a swampy region on the coast of Tuscany
marl: earth
meed: a reward or recompense
mere: a lake or marsh
midge: a gnatlike insect
mirific: wondrous
moiling: 1) toiling; 2) confused
moly: an imaginary herb
momently: 1) from moment to moment; 2) at any moment
mordant: biting, caustic
mortise: to join securely
mummia: var. of *mummy*
murex: a sea mussel
murkness: gloom
must (n.): staleness
mysteriarch: one who presides over mysteries
nacred: covered with nacre (mother-of-pearl)
nard: ointment made from the nard plant
nathless: nevertheless
necrophore: a type of beetle
nemoral: pertaining to a grove
nenuphar: a water-lily
nepenthe: an imaginary drug to induce forgetfulness
nurstle: to nuzzle
occlusion: a shutting or blocking
octireme: a ship with eight ranks of oars
orichalc[um]: a kind of brass
orris: the fleur-de-lys
ort: a fragment of food left after a meal
ostent: a sign or portent
oubliette: a concealed dungeon
paladin: a knight
palfray: var. of *palfrey* (a saddle-horse)
Paphos: island in the Aegean Sea; reputed home of Aphrodite
parapegm: a tablet bearing a proclamation
pard: a leopard or panther
parhelion: a bright spot of light seen on the ring of a solar halo
parterre: a flower garden arranged in sections

patchouli: a perfume made from the patchouli plant
pavonine: pertaining to the peacock
pellucid: exceptionally clear
peridoz: chrysolite
phare: a lighthouse
pitter: to make a repetitive sound
planish: to smooth or polish by hammering or rolling
plenilune: the full moon
predal: predatory
primogeniture: the right of the eldest son to inherit his father's estate
prore: the prow of a ship
provender: food or provisions
purfle: to decorate the border of
queach: a dense growth of bushes
quickening: to give life to; to rouse
raddle: to interweave
ravin: a plundering
recondite: obscure
relume: to light again
reptant: creeping
revenant: ghost; that which returns from the dead
rivelled: wrinkled or furrowed
romaunt: a romantic story or poem
rondure: roundness
rutilance: a reddish glow
Rutilicus: a name for the star Beta Herculis
Saiph: a name for the star Kappa Orionis
santal: sandalwood
sard: a variety of chalcedony
sate: archaic past participle of *sit*
scaur: a cliff
scolopendra: a fabulous fish
selenic: pertaining to the moon
sendaline: pertaining to sendal (a light silk fabric)
senescent: aging
seneschal: the manager of the domestic affairs of a medieval noble
Set: the brother and slayer of Osiris in Egyptian mythology
shoon: archaic plural of *shoe*
sidereal: pertaining to the stars
similor: a kind of yellow brass
simoon: a hot, sand-laden wind

simorgh: a monstrous bird capable of speech
sough: a soft murmuring sound
strait: narrow
suzerain: a sovereign
syrt: quicksand
Tellurian: pertaining to the earth
teraphim: idols or monsters (plural only)
tetter: any of a group of skin diseases (herpes, eczema, etc.)
threne: a dirge
throeless: without a spasm
thurifer: an acolyte who carries a thurible (censer)
thyrse: a staff (as carried by Dionysus)
tragelaphous: pertaining to a fictitious compound of goat and stag
transplendent: brilliantly translucent
trinal: threefold
typhon: a whirlwind or hurricane
Typhonian: pertaining to Typhon, the father of winds in Greek mythology
unceremented: lacking a shroud
undine: a water-sprite
unguerdoned: lacking a reward
unwildered: not lost
usance: use
vair: a fur used on the hem of robes
vatic: pertaining to prophecy
vaticination: prophecy
venefic: poisonous
verge: edge, boundary
vermeil: vermilion
vespertine: pertaining to the evening
weft: the yarns carried back and forth across the warp in weaving
weld: the joint formed by welding
welkin: the sky
whiffle: to blow fitfully; to vacillate
whilom: formerly
wivern (wyver, wyvern): a two-legged winged dragon
wold: a treeless plain
wot: to know
ziggurat: a temple tower
Zimimar: imaginary realm invented by CAS
zone: a belt or girdle

BIBLIOGRAPHY

This bibliography consists primarily of first appearances in magazines (all appearances in *WT* are given) and all appearances in collections of Smith's poems. Poems printed in book reviews are not cited, nor are appearances in anthologies (unless a first appearance) nor reprints from books. The following abbreviations are used:

AJ   *Auburn Journal* (newspaper)
DC   *The Dark Chateau* (Sauk City, WI: Arkham House, December 1951)
EC   *Ebony and Crystal* (Auburn, CA: Auburn Journal, December 1922)
HD   *The Hill of Dionysus* (Glendale, CA: Roy A. Squires, November 1962)
Nero   *Nero and Other Poems* (Lakeport, CA: The Futile Press, May 1937)
OS   *Odes and Sonnets* (San Francisco: Book Club of California, June 1918)
S   *Sandalwood* (Auburn, CA: Auburn Journal, October 1925)
S&P   *Spells and Philtres* (Sauk City, WI: Arkham House, March 1958)
SP   *Selected Poems* (Sauk City, WI: Arkham House, November 1971)
ST   *The Star-Treader and Other Poems* (San Francisco: A. M. Robertson, November 1912)
WT   *Weird Tales* (magazine)

The Abyss Triumphant: *Town Talk,* No. 1041 (3 August 1912): 8; in *EC* and *SP*.

Adventure: *AJ* 24, No. 18 (14 February 1924; 30 lines only): 6; in *S* and *SP*.

After Armageddon: *Recluse* (1927): 15; in *SP*.

Alienage: *AJ* 23, No. 38 (5 July 1923): 6; *Wanderer* 1, No. 6 (November 1923): 4–5; in *S* and *SP*.

Amithaine: *Different* 7, No. 3 (Autumn 1951): 9; in *DC*. Written 21 October 1950.

The Ancient Quest: In *A Song from Hell* (Glendale, CA: Roy A. Squires, 1975).

Antepast: In *EC* (as "Anticipation") and *SP*.

Atlantis: In *ST* and *SP*.

Averoigne: *Challenge* (Spring 1951); in *DC*.

Averted Malefice: In *ST* and *SP*.

Bacchante: *WT* 34, No. 6 (December 1939): 84; in *SP* and *HD*.

Beyond the Great Wall: *Asia* 24, No. 5 (May 1924): 359; in *EC* and *SP*. Written 21 December 1919.

Cambion: In *SP* and *DC*. First title: "The Unnamed."

Canticle: In *SP*.

The Castle of Dreams: In *The Potion of Dreams* (Glendale, CA: Roy A. Squires, 1975).

Chance: *AJ* 23, No. 35 (14 June 1923): 6; *Bloodstone* 1, No. 2 (November 1937): 4; in *SP*.

The City in the Desert: In *EC* and *SP*.

The City of Destruction: *Arkham Sampler* 1, No. 1 (Winter 1948): 22; in *SP*.

The City of the Titans: *Challenge* (Fall 1950); in *SP*.

Cleopatra: In *EC* and *SP*. First title: "Anthony to Cleopatra."

The Cloud-Islands: In *ST*.

Connaissance: In *SP*. Written 26 January 1929.

Cycles: *In Memoriam: Clark Ashton Smith* (Baltimore: Mirage Press, 1963) and *The Black Book of Clark Ashton Smith* (Sauk City, WI: Arkham House, 1979). Written 4 June 1961; Smith's last poem.

The Dark Chateau: In *DC*. Written c. 1950.

A Dead City: In *ST* and *SP*.

Desert Dweller: *WT* 36, No. 12 (July 1943): 71; in *SP* and *DC*. Written 13 August 1937.

Desire of Vastness: In *EC* and *SP*.

Desolation: In *EC* and *SP*.

Dissonance: *Thrill Book* 2, No. 6 (15 September 1919): 149; in *EC* and *SP*.

Dolor of Dreams: *AJ* 23, No. 46 (30 August 1923): 6; in *SP*.

The Dream-Bridge: In *ST*.

The Dream-God's Realm: In *The Potion of Dreams* (Glendale, CA: Roy A. Squires, 1975).

A Dream of Beauty: *Academy* 81 (12 August 1911): 196; in *ST, Nero,* and *SP*.

A Dream of Oblivion: In *The Potion of Dreams* (Glendale, CA: Roy A. Squires, 1975).

A Dream of the Abyss: *Fantasy Fan* 1, No. 3 (November 1933): 41; in *SP*.

Echo of Memnon: In *EC* and *SP*.

The Eldritch Dark: In *ST, Nero,* and *SP*.

Enchanted Mirrors: *AJ* 26, No. 4 (5 November 1925): 4; in *S* and *SP*.

Ennui: *WT* 27, No. 5 (May 1936): 547; in *S* and *SP*. A recasting of the sonnet "Ennui" (alternate title: "The Ennuyé"; *AJ* 25, No. 14 [15 January 1925]: 5) in alexandrines. Written c. December 1935.

The Envoys: *AJ* 26, 13 (7 January 1926): 4; *Overland Monthly and Out West Magazine* 84, No. 6 (July 1926): 230 (to supersede the severely misprinted version in June 1926); in *SP*.

Exorcism: In *SP*. Written 17 January 1929.

Exotique: In *OS, EC,* and *SP*.

Fantasie d'Antan: [= "Fantasy of Antan"] *WT* 14, No. 6 (December 1929): 724; in *SP*.

Farewell to Eros: *WT* 31, No. 6 (June 1938): 759; in *SP* and *S&P*.

The Flight of Azrael: *Fantastic Worlds* (Summer 1952); in *SP*.

Forgotten Sorrow: *AJ* 23, No. 42 (2 August 1923): 6; in *S* and *SP*.

The Funeral Urn: *AJ* 23, No. 45 (23 August 1923): 6; in *SP*.

The Ghoul and the Seraph: In *EC* and *SP*.

H. P. L.: In H. P. Lovecraft and others, *The Shuttered Room and Other Pieces* (Sauk City, WI: Arkham House, 1959). Written 17 June 1959.

The Hashish-Eater; or, The Apocalypse of Evil: In *EC* and *SP*. Written c. 20 February 1920.

The Hill of Dionysus: In *SP* and *HD*. Written 5 November 1942.

The Hope of the Infinite: In *EC* and *SP*.

Imagination: Previously unpublished.

In Lemuria: *Lyric West* 4, No. 1 (July–August 1921): 6; in *EC* and *SP*.

In Saturn: *Sonnet* 2, No. 2 (January–February 1919): 2; in *EC* and *SP*.

In Slumber: *WT* 24, No. 2 (August 1934): 253; in *SP*. Written c. January 1934.

In the Desert: In *SP*.

In Thessaly: *WT* 26, No. 5 (November 1935): 551; in *SP*. Written 24 May 1935.

The Incubus of Time: *Fire and Sleet and Candlelight,* ed. August Derleth (Sauk City, WI: Arkham House, 1961); in *SP*.

Inferno: In *EC* and *SP*. Written 24 April 1918.

Interrogation: *WT* 10, No. 3 (September 1927): 414; in *S* and *SP*. Written 14 September 1925.

Jungle Twilight: *Oriental Stories* 2, No. 3 (Summer 1932): 420 (15 lines only); in *SP* and *S&P*.

The Kingdom of Shadows: In *EC* and *SP*.

Lament of the Stars: In *ST*.

Lamia: *Arkham Sampler* 1, No. 1 (Winter 1948): [20]; in *SP*. Written 24 January 1940.

The Land of Evil Stars: In *EC* and *SP*.

The Last Goddess: In *SP*.

The Last Night: In *ST* and *SP*.

The Last Oblivion: *AJ* 24, No. 17 (7 February 1924): 6; in *S* and *SP*.

Laus Mortis: [= "The Praise of Death"] *Pearson's Magazine* 47, No. 3 (September 1921): 100. In *EC* and *SP*.

Lethe: In *ST* and *SP*.

Love Malevolent: In *EC*.

Luna Aeternalis: *WT* 42, No. 4 (May 1950): 43; in *SP* and *DC*. Written 1912; revised 1948.

Lunar Mystery: In *S* and *SP*. Written 1915. First title: "Dream-Mystery."

Maya: *AJ* 25, No. 23 (19 March 1925): 4; *Step-Ladder* 13, No. 5 (May 1927): 135; in *S* and *SP*.

Medusa: In *ST, Nero,* and *SP*. Written 17 May 1911.

The Medusa of Despair: *Town Talk* No. 1113 (20 December 1913): 8; in *OS, EC,* and *SP*.

The Medusa of the Skies: In *ST* and *SP*

The Melancholy Pool: In *EC* and *SP;* also in *WT* 3, No. 3 (March 1924): 21.

Memnon at Midnight: In *OS, EC,* and *SP*. In *OS* and *EC,* dedicated to Albert M[aurice] Bender (1866–1941), benefactor and friend of Smith.

Midnight Beach: *Wings* 6, No.7 (May 1944): 14; in *SP* and *HD*. Written 5 September 1943.

Minatory: *AJ* 25, No. 29 (30 April 1925): 6; *Raven* 2, No. 3 (Autumn 1944): 17; in *S* and *SP*.

Le Miroir des blanches fleurs: [= "The Mirror of White Flowers"] An English translation of Smith's poem in French (in *SP*). Previously unpublished.

Moon-Dawn: *WT* 2, No. 1 (July–August 1923): 48 (as "The Red Moon"); *AJ* 24, No. 15 (24 January 1924): 6 (as "The Red Moon"); in *S* and *SP*.

The Moonlight Desert: Previously unpublished.

Mors: In *SP*. Written 24 April 1918. First title: "Anodyne."

The Motes: In *EC* and *SP*.

The Mummy: *Sonnet* 3, No. 4 (May–June 1919): 3; in *EC*. Written in 1915.

The Nameless Wraith: *Arkham Sampler* 1, No. 1 (Winter 1948): 21; in *SP* and *S&P*.

Necromancy: *Fantasy Fan* 1, No. 12 (August 1934): 188; *WT* 36, No. 10 (March 1943): 105; in *SP*. Written c. January 1934.

The Nereid: *Yale Review* 2 No. 4: (July 1913): 685–6; in *EC* and *SP*. Written before 12 January 1913.

Nero: In *ST, OS, Nero,* and *SP.* Written in April 1912.

Nightmare: In *EC* and *SP.*

The Nightmare Tarn: *WT* 14, No. 5 (November 1929): 624; in *SP.*

Nirvana: In *ST* and *SP.*

Not Theirs the Cypress-Arch: *Wings* 10, No. 4 (Winter 1952): 13; in *S&P.* Written 12 January 1951.

Nyctalops: *WT* 14, No. 4 (October 1929): 516; in *SP.*

Ode on Imagination: In *ST* and *SP.*

Ode to Light: In *The Titans in Tartarus* (Glendale, CA: Roy A. Squires, 1974).

Ode to Matter: In *The Tartarus of the Suns* (Glendale, CA: Roy A. Squires, 1970).

Ode to the Abyss: In *SP, OS,* and *SP.* Written 3 May 1911.

Omniety: *Raven* 1, No. 4 (Winter 1944): 21; in *SP* and *HD.*

On Re-reading Baudelaire: *AJ* 24, No. 9 (13 December 1923): 6; in *S* and *SP.* First title, "On Reading Baudelaire."

Ougabalys: *WT* 15, No. 1 (January 1930): 135. Written 15 September 1929. Later revised as "Tolometh" (*SP*).

The Outer Land: *Supramundane Stories Quarerly* 1, No. 2 (Spring 1937) (as "Alienation"); *Spearhead* 2, 2 (Spring 1951): 3–5; in *SP* and *DC.* Written 26 May 1935.

Outlanders: In *Nero*; *WT* 31, No. 6 (June 1938): 746; in *SP.* Written c. July 1937. The appearance in *WT* is dedicated to David Warren Ryder (1892–1975), author of "The Price of Poetry," *Controversy* (December 1934); rpt. by the Futile Press (June 1937) and laid in CAS's *Nero.*

Pour Chercher du nouveau: [= "In Search of the New"] *Arkham Sampler* No. 8 (Autumn 1949): 28–29; in *SP* and *DC.*

The Power of Eld: In *The Tartarus of the Suns* (Glendale, CA: Roy A. Squires, 1970).

The Prophet Speaks: *WT* 32, No. 3 (September 1938): 348; in *SP* and *S&P.*

The Pursuer: *Portals* (November 1957). In *SP.*

The Refuge of Beauty: *L'Alouette* 1, No. 3 (May 1924): 66. In *OS, EC,* and *SP.*

Remembered Light: *Poetry* 1, No. 3 (December 1912): 78; in *EC* and *SP.*

Resurrection: *WT* 39, No. 11 (July 1947): 85. In *SP* and *HD.*

Retrospect and Forecast: In *ST, Nero,* and *SP.* Written 10 January 1912.

The Return of Hyperion: In *ST* and *SP.*

Revenant: *Fantasy Fan* 1, No. 7 (March 1934): 106–7; in *SP.* Written c. July 1933.

Rosa Mystica: *Lyric West* 1, No. 8 (December 1921): 7; in *EC* and *SP.*

Said the Dreamer: *Vortex* 1, No. 2 (1947); in *SP* and *S&P*.

Sandalwood: *Leaves* No. 1 (Summer 1937): 49. Smith's original prologue to *S*.

Satan Unrepentant: In *OS*, *EC*, and *SP*. Written in October 1912.

Saturn: In *ST* and *SP*.

The Saturnienne: *WT* 10, No. 6 (December 1927): 728; in *SP*. Written before Christmas 1925.

Selenique: *AJ* 23, No. 41 (26 July 1923): 6 (as "Simile"); in *S* and *SP*.

September: In *SP*. Written 11 September 1929.

Shadow of Nightmare: In *ST* and *SP*.

Shadows: *WT* 15, No. 2 (February 1930): 154; in *SP*. Written 12 September 1929.

Soliloquy in a Ebon Tower: In *DC*.

Solution: *WT* 3, No. 1 (January 1924): 32; in *EC* and *SP*.

Some Blind Eidolon: *Kaleidograph* 19, No. 2 (June 1947): 2; in *SP* and *DC*. Written 23 March 1942.

A Song from Hell: In *A Song from Hell* (Glendale, CA: Roy A. Squires, 1975).

The Song of a Comet: In *ST*, *Nero*, and *SP*.

A Song of Dreams: In *ST*, *Nero*, and *SP*.

Song of the Necromancer: *WT* 29, No. 2 (February 1937): 220; in *SP*.

The Sorcerer to His Love: *WT* 39, No. 1 (September 1945): 63; in *SP* and *HD*. Written 16 November 1941.

The Star-Treader: In *ST* and *SP*. Written in September or October 1911.

Strangeness: *Bohemia* 2, No. 4 ([May] 1917): 3; in *EC* and *SP*. Written 3 October 1916.

Symbols: *London Mercury* No. 33 (July 1922): 245; in *EC* and *SP*.

The Tears of Lilith: In *EC* and *SP*. Written 26 April 1917.

The Titans in Tartarus: In *The Titans in Tartarus* (Glendale, CA: Roy A. Squires, 1974).

To Antares: In *SP*. Written 25 August 1927.

To George Sterling: A Valediction: *The Overland Monthly and Out West Magazine* 85, No. 11 (November 1927): 338. In *SP*. Written December 1926.

To Howard Phillips Lovecraft: *WT* 30, No. 1 (July 1937): 48; in *SP*. Written 31 March 1937, sixteen days after Lovecraft's death.

To Nora May French: In *EC* and *SP*. Begun c. June 1916 but not completed until July 1920 (see Smith to Sterling, 20 June 1916, 20 July 1920).

To Omar Khayyam: *Lyric West* 5, No. 8 (May–June 1926): 216–17. In *EC* and *SP*. Written 13 December 1919. First title: "To Omar."

To the Chimera: *AJ* 24, No. 25 (3 April 1924):6; *United Amateur* 23, No. 1 (May 1924): 7; *WT* 40, No. 6 (September 1948): 79; in *S* and *SP*.

To the Daemon of Sublimity: *Fire and Sleet and Candlelight,* ed. August Derleth (Sauk City, WI: Arkham House, 1961); in *SP*.

To the Darkness: In *ST, OS, Nero,* and *SP*.

Transcendence: In *EC* and *SP*.

Triple Aspect: In *EC* and *SP*.

Twilight on the Snow: In *EC* and *SP*.

The Twilight Woods: In *The Fanes of Dawn* (Glendale, CA: Roy A. Squires, 1976).

A Vision of Lucifer: In *EC* and *SP*.

Warning: *WT* 12, No. 4 (October 1928): 525; in *SP*. Written 3 March 1928.

The Whisper of the Worm: In *SP* (presented as a translation of the mythical poet Christophe des Laurières).

White Death: In *ST* and *SP*.

The Wingless Archangels: *AJ* 23, No. 37 (28 June 1923): 6; in *S* and *SP*.

Witch-Dance: *WT* 36, No. 1 (September 1941): 104; in *SP* and *HD*.

The Witch in the Graveyard: In *EC* and *SP*.

The Witch with Eyes of Amber: *AJ* 23, No. 32 (24 May 1923): 6; *Epos* 1, No. 4 (Summer 1950): 14; in *SP* and *DC*. First title: "The Witch with the Heart of Amber."

Zothique: In *DC*.

Additional information about the publication of Smith's work may be found in Donald Sidney-Fryer et al., *Emperor of Dreams: A Clark Ashton Smith Bibiliography* (West Kingston, RI: Donald M. Grant, 1978).

Index of Titles

The Abyss Triumphant 41
Adventure 136
After Armageddon 44
Alienage 135
Amithaine 109
The Ancient Quest 45
Antepast 159
Atlantis 89
Averoigne 111
Averted Malefice 52
Bacchante 143
Beyond the Great Wall 93
Cambion 77
Canticle 138
The Castle of Dreams 114
Chance 79
The City in the Desert 95
The City of Destruction 92
The City of the Titans 92
Cleopatra 132
The Cloud-Islands 91
Connaissance 139
Cycles 174
The Dark Chateau 110
A Dead City 90
Desert Dweller 108
Desire of Vastness 42
Desolation 155
Dissonance 156
Dolor of Dreams 121
The Dream-Bridge 120
The Dream-God's Realm 114
A Dream of Beauty 152
A Dream of Oblivion 47
A Dream of the Abyss 43
Echo of Memnon 123
The Eldritch Dark 89
Enchanted Mirrors 125

Ennui 162
The Envoys 73
Exorcism 139
Exotique 131
Fantaisie d'Antan 127
Farewell to Eros 141
The Flight of Azrael 70
The Funeral Urn 160
Forgotten Sorrow 159
The Ghoul and the Seraph 63
The Hashish-Heater; or, The Apocalypse of Evil 15
H. P. L. 171
The Hill of Dionysus 145
The Hope of the Infinite 158
Imagination 115
In Lemuria 60
In Saturn 40
In Slumber 128
In the Desert 153
In Thessaly 105
The Incubus of Time 157
Inferno 156
Interrogation 137
Jungle Twilight 76
The Kingdom of Shadows 98
Lament of the Stars 38
Lamia 140
The Land of Evil Stars 97
The Last Goddess 124
The Last Night 118
The Last Oblivion 134
Laus Mortis 158
Lethe 89
Love Malevolent 124
Luna Aeternalis 122
Lunar Mystery 160
Maya 126
Medusa 51
The Medusa of Despair 67
The Medusa of the Skies 53
The Melancholy Pool 96
Memnon at Midnight 98
Midnight Beach 147
Minatory 72

Le Miroir des blanches fleurs 106
Moon-Dawn 100
The Moonlight Desert 107
Mors 161
The Motes 41
The Mummy 71
The Nameless Wraith 154
Necromancy 76
The Nereid 130
Nero 49
Nightmare 123
The Nightmare Tarn 101
Nirvana 35
Not Theirs the Cypress-Arch 84
Nyctalops 74
Ode on Imagination 149
Ode to Light 46
Ode to Matter 47
Ode to the Abyss 33
Omniety 147
On Re-reading Baudelaire 167
Ougabalys 107
The Outer Land 103
Outlanders 100
Pour chercher du nouveau 82
The Power of Eld 129
The Prophet Speaks 102
The Pursuer 153
The Refuge of Beauty 133
Remembered Light 156
Resurrection 144
Retrospect and Forecast 151
Revenant 79
Rosa Mystica 94
Said the Dreamer 120
Sandalwood 133
Satan Unrepentant 60
Saturn 53
The Saturnienne 78
Selenique 126
September 161
Shadow of Nightmare 118
Shadows 42
Soliloquy in a Ebon Tower 171

Solution 94
Some Blind Eidolon 142
A Song from Hell 85
The Song of a Comet 36
A Song of Dreams 119
Song of the Necromancer 81
The Sorcerer to His Love 145
The Star-Treader 30
Strangeness 129
Symbols 95
The Tears of Lilith 132
The Titans in Tartarus 86
To Antares 138
To George Sterling: A Valediction 168
To Howard Phillips Lovecraft 170
To Nora May French 165
To Omar Khayyam 163
To the Chimera 72
To the Daemon of Sublimity 155
To the Darkness 151
Transcendence 131
Triple Aspect 40
Twilight on the Snow 96
The Twilight Woods 88
A Vision of Lucifer 67
Warning 101
The Whisper of the Worm 73
White Death 90
The Wingless Archangels 125
The Witch in the Graveyard 68
The Witch with Eyes of Amber 77
Witch-Dance 83
Zothique 112

INDEX OF FIRST LINES

A crownless king who reigns alone, 98
A stranger grief than any grief by music told 159
A voice came to me from the night, and said, 119
A voice cried to me in a dawn of dreams, 30
Above its domes the gulfs accumulate. 89
Above the desert's dark-obscured expanse 107
All drear and barren seemed the hours, 120
Antares, star of memory, 138
As drear and barren as the glooms of Death, 51
As eve to purple turns the afterglow 88
As one who seeks the silver moth of night 154
As though a thousand vampires, from the day 123
Before the hill's high altar bowed, 96
Beneath my dome of sleep, secure-immersed 129
Beneath the skies of Saturn, pale and many-mooned, 78
Between the windy, swirling fire 83
Beyond the bourn of dreams, their fortunate sphere, 125
Beyond the far Cathayan wall 93
Bow down before the daemon of the world— 79
Bow down: I am the emperor of dreams; 15
By an alien dream despatched and driven 122
By desert-deepened wells and chasmed ways, 100
Call up the lordly daemon that in Cimmeria dwells 82
City forbanned by seer and god and devil! 102
Climbing from out what nadir-fountained sea, 153
Dear one, what do we here? 135
Dream not the dead will wait, 84
Farewell, a late farewell! Tearless and unforgetting, 168
Fools of the world, who dream that dreams are true— 126
Forgetting still what holier lilies bloom 167
From out the light of many a mightier day, 71
From regions of the sun's half-dreamt decay, 133
From teak and tamarind and palm 76
From the close valleys of thy love, 103
God walks lightly in the gardens of a cold, dark star, 44
Grey hells, or hells aglow with hot and scarlet flowers; 156
Hast heard the voices of the fen, 100
He who trod the shadows of Zothique 112

Her face the sinking stars desire: 130
How long, O soul, hast parleyed with the worm— 73
I am that spawn of witch and demon 77
I am the master of strange spells 147
I am the spectre who returns 79
I dreamed a dream: I stood upon a height, 118
I dreamed that each most lovely, perfect thing 152
I fain would love thee, but thy lips are fed 124
I flow beneath the columns that upbear 89
I may not mask for ever with the grace 67
I met a witch with amber eyes 77
I met the night in unfamiliar lands, 153
I sat beside the moonless tarn alone, 101
I saw a city in a lonely land; 92
I saw a shape with human form and face, 67
I saw a universe today: 41
I seemed at the sheer end: 43
I wandered down Sleep's vast and sunless vale, 114
I wandered ere the dream was done 123
I wane and weary: come, thou swifter One, 155
I will repeat a subtle rune— 81
Ill days and dolorous nights and years accurst— 157
Imagination, to thine occult sight, 115
Imagination's eyes 149
Importunate, the lion-throated sea, 165
In a lost land, that only dreams have known, 95
In Averoigne the enchantress weaves 111
In billow-lost Poseidonis 107
In my heart a wizard book, 138
In starlight, by the ghostly sea, 147
It lies beyond the farthest sea, 114
It seems to me that I have lived alone— 155
Let us leave the hateful town 136
Like a worm-fretted visage from the tomb, 53
Like ghosts returning stealthily 139
Lo, for Earth's manifest monotony 40
Longer ago than Eden's oldest morn, 142
Lord of the many pangs, the single ecstasy! 141
Lost and alien lie the leas, 127
Lost from those archangelic thrones that star, 60
Love, will you look with me 137
Lover of hills and fields and towns antique, 170
Low in the far-flung shadow of the world, 86
Marked by that priesthood of the Night's misrule, 96

Men say the gods have flown; 143
Methought the world was bound with final frost: 90
Methought upon the tomb-encumbered shore 98
My dreams were nests of horror, whimsey-wrought 120
My heart is like some onyx urn 160
My heart is made a necromancer's glass, 76
My hope is in the unharvestable deep 158
'Neath blue days, and gold, and green, 97
No more of gold and marble, nor of snow 95
None other saw them when they came 73
Not while the woods are redolent with spring, 134
Now as the twilight's doubtful interval 89
Now were the Titans gathered round their king 53
O giant stars, born of eternal night, 45
O love, thy lips are bright and cold, 129
O lovely demon, half-divine! 132
O many-gulfed, unalterable one, 33
O tissued fabric of the frame of things, 47
O'er gardens lulled with ghostly light 159
Omar, within thy scented garden-close, 163
One tone is mute within the starry singing, 38
Only through the senses have I known you, 139
Out of the desert lair the lamia came, 140
Outside the time-dimension, and outside 171
Pale plummet of the stark immensities, 36
Perfect, marmoreal, curved and carven statue-wise, 126
Poised as a god whose lone, detachèd post, 35
Remember thou the tarn whose water once allured us 106
Rememberest thou? Enormous gongs of stone 60
Scorners of the Muse, beware! 72
Sit, sister, now that haggish Hecate 68
Slumberously burns the sun 161
Sorceress and sorcerer, 144
Supreme with night, what high mysteriarch— 42
Sweeter the thought of death to me 161
The day of Time was darkening to its end: 45
The force of suns had waned beyond recall. 41
The ghostly fire that walks the fen, 94
The harsh, brief sob of broken horns; the sound 156
The hills, a-throng with swarthy pine, 100
The imperishable phantoms, Love and Fame, 158
The incognizable kings of Night, within their unrevealed abyss, 92
The lamp burns stilly in the standing air, 171
The mysteries of your former dust, 110

The Pestilence is on the wing! 63
The secret rose we vainly dream to find 94
The shadow of a sorrow haunts the light, 121
The sorcerer departs . . . and his high tower is drowned 174
The stench of stagnant waters broke my dream, 128
The thought of death to me 159
The years are a falling of snow, 156
There is no room in any town (he said) 108
These are enchanted mirrors that I bring, 125
This is enchanted ground 145
This Rome, that was the toil of many men, 49
This song I got me from the nether pits, 85
Thou art immured in some sad garden sown with dust 162
Thou hast taken the light of many suns, 151
Thy beauty is the warmth and languor of an orient autumn, 132
Thy mouth is like a crimson orchid-flower 131
Thy shadow falls on the fount, 42
To laud the loves of old, 124
To look on love with disenamored eyes; 131
Turn round, O Life, and know with eyes aghast 151
Twilight ascends the abandoned ramps of noon 90
Unknown chimera, take us, for we tire 72
Upon the seas of Saturn I have sailed 40
Upon thy separate road 133
What gulf-ascended hand is this, that grips 118
What islands marvellous are these, 91
What sky beheld thy primal birth, 46
What world is this, all desolate and dim 70
When I lay dead in Thessaly, 105
Where mandrakes, crying from the moonless fen, 52
Who has seen the towers of Amithaine 109
Within your arms I will forget 145
Ye that see in darkness 74